Sleigh the Night

LADY MARIE

CONTENTS

TROPES, CONTENT WARNINGS + MORE

Sleigh the Night is a Black romantic erotica collection made up of three short stories set in the fictional small mountain town of Aurora Ridge. The events of these stories take place over one weekend between a group of friends trapped in a cabin by a snowstorm. Each story in this collection takes place simultaneously and focuses on a different couple, but should be read in the order they're presented. Don't worry, it all comes together in the end, so enjoy the ride.

The characters featured in these stories are also featured in the prequel novella *After Tonight*, which details the start of Deziree and Izaiah's relationship. While *Sleigh the Night* can be read as a standalone, starting with *After Tonight* provides a fuller reading experience. If you decide you'd like to dive into *After Tonight* first, you can click HERE or scan the QR code below.

TROPES

Vacation romance, small town, forced proximity, Black romance, best friend's ex, best friend's brother, brother's best friend, annoyance to lovers, accidental pregnancy, forbidden romance, childhood friends to lovers, one night stand turned more

TAGS

Holiday erotica, MF, multiple POVS, "trapped in a snowstorm with the person I'm not supposed to want, HELP!", not-so-one night stand, plus-size FMCs, asshole MMC, cinnamon roll MMCs, hand necklaces, "I'm not supposed to want you, but I do", warm nights and snowball fights, sex toys, cumming on the mountain, fast burn

CONTENT WARNINGS

This collection features content and themes throughout that may not be suitable for all readers. This includes, but is not limited to adult language, recreational alcohol consumption, explicit sexual content, semi-public sex acts, pregnancy and brief mentions of abortion.

As with all Lady Marie projects, please read with care.

For anyone who's ever wanted what they shouldn't have...and went for it anyway

Trina

| FRIDAY |

I'M *a real messy bitch who lives for drama.*

My favorite scammer really ate with that line because it described me perfectly. You wouldn't be able to guess it by looking at me. Hell, spend a few hours with me and you still might not figure it out, but it's the only explanation for the fucking mess I'd found myself in.

'Cause who else but a messy bitch would agree to being stuck in a cabin, a snowstorm on the way, with a nigga she'd had sex with and ghosted almost two months ago sleeping right down the hall?

A nigga who, I might add, also happened to be her best friend's ex?

Yeah, like I said: Grade-A messy bitch status.

To my credit, I didn't *know* there was the potential for us to get trapped up here. Had there been snow in the forecast? Sure.

Did the idea of a winter wonderland just before the holidays sound amazing? Absolutely.

But nobody said anything about a goddamn blizzard. Not to mention the last I'd heard, Matt had canceled because of some big work project, which was the only reason I'd even agreed to come in the first place.

Wait, no, that was a lie.

Dezireé put this trip together back in September, at least three weeks before Matt and I slept together. Back when my brain understood I could look but not touch because he was off-limits. Unfortunately, I managed to forget that for about three days, and by the time I remembered, backing out wasn't an option. My besties weren't having it. No matter what excuse I came up with, Kamille and Dezireé stepped right over it. Maybe it was my fault for telling them I had so much unused PTO saved up, my boss was practically shoving me out the door begging me to take a vacation.

Me and my big fucking mouth.

So yeah, because my weak ass didn't know how to keep my mouth—*or my legs*—shut, here I was on the most awkward trip imaginable.

"Fix your face," Kamille said as we shuffled around the kitchen putting groceries away while the guys unloaded the rest of the bags from the truck. We'd made the trip to the grocery store earlier than planned because of the weather, and for that, I was silently grateful...for my own personal reasons.

"There's nothing wrong with my face."

"Survey says that's a lie," she cackled, slipping into the walk-in pantry and slipping out just as quickly. "I can't decide whether your face is sour as shit or you look like a deer caught in headlights, but it's been going on for the last three hours."

She stopped, leaning against the kitchen island and snagging a chip from the bag she'd opened in the car. "Maybe you should just tell me what the issue is."

"There's no issue, Kami." I did my best not to look at her. One look and she'd immediately know I was lying. Being an honest person was supposed to be a commendable trait, but moments like these made me wish I'd picked up some version of the skill.

"I mean, there shouldn't be. You got to sit in the back with the sweetest, most mild-mannered, and reliable person we know. Meanwhile, I had to ride in the front seat for four hours with Satan. If anyone should be complaining, it's me."

Kamille's ability to invoke just the right amount of drama was exactly why she made the perfect kindergarten teacher. The kids probably ate it up.

"No one is complaining except for *you*, Kami." Talking about her never-ending hatred for Grayson wasn't high up on the list of things I wanted to do right now, but it was infinitely better than talking about my face or the anxiety I'd spent all day trying to hide.

"And I should be! That asshole is so lucky I love his sister, otherwise my foot would be so far up his ass he'd have toes for teeth."

I'd heard that once...or twice...or fifty times. And every time was funnier than the last.

"Yeah, laugh it up. And while you're over there laughing, explain to me what's got your panties in a bunch. I saw your nose in your work phone the whole ride. Didn't we tell you to leave that thing at home? Now look, all that working has your ass acting as funky as Grayson's draws."

"Ewww, now see that's nasty."

"Just like him."

I laughed harder as I shook my head. "Alright, friend, I get it!"

Why was she like this? Kamille hated that man's guts and none of us knew why. Well, Grayson probably did, but he wasn't saying anything about it. He'd much rather spend his time egging her on. Anytime we asked her about it, she'd just say he gave the world plenty of reasons to hate his ass so why did she have to settle on just one.

"Yeah, okay. You just make sure that phone stays in the bag for the next few days."

If only the answers to my problems were that simple. If all it took was turning off a damn phone to fix my mood, I would have done it a long time ago. This was a lot more complicated. My problem and I were about to be sleeping under the same roof.

With his ex and her new man.

But since I couldn't actually say that to Kamille, I pulled her into a hug instead and promised that I wouldn't so much as spell the word *work* for the rest of the weekend.

She turned her nose up. "That's more like it. I would hate to have to drop you like a bad habit friend. You're lucky I like my women fine with an attitude."

"That makes two of us," a voice said. Now it was Kami's turn to put on her stank face.

"Do not start with me, Grayson." Her teeth were gritted as she narrowed her eyes on him, the disgust and agitation written all over her face.

That man is absolutely about to start.

"Damn, a nigga can't agree with you? I thought women loved it when you told them they were right."

I was doing everything I could not to snicker at the way he was purposely trying to get on her nerves. It was obvious he was getting a kick out of it too. Grayson loved getting under Kamille's skin and I'd bet money he planned on fucking with her the entire time we were in Aurora Ridge. This cute mountain town might not be big enough for them, let alone this cabin.

Honestly, when Deziree said he was coming too, I was shocked that Kami even agreed to come. Then again, she was never one to turn down a vacation, so I guess she thought dealing with him was a small price to pay. She may have misjudged that one.

"Are they going to be like this all weekend?" The way the words caressed my ear sent shivers down my spine.

Or maybe just knowing its owner was so close to me was enough to cause a reaction.

"Probably," I said, clearing my throat and trying to put some space between us. "I'm assuming y'all got everything out the car."

"Yep, all the bags are in the front hallway."

Stepping away was a mistake. The only thing worse than having Matthew in my personal space was having him out of it because now, I had no choice but to actually look at him.

I could've sworn light-skinned men were out of season, but clearly no one told him because there he stood, looking just as fine as ever, if not more so. Chiseled jaw, green eyes with a hint of gray when the light hit them just right, muscles that even now —when they were hidden under that gray quarter-zip turtleneck —seemed to bulge and flex and beg for my attention, topped off with a grown ass goatee framing a boyish grin like the one he was giving me now. Matthew was one of those men who no one could ever accuse of being ugly, no matter what their type was. And that in itself was the problem.

"Thanks."

"Don't mention it."

We stood there in awkward silence, the sounds of Kamille and Grayson bickering behind us.

Were they actually further away or was his presence just overwhelming my senses?

"Trin—"

Nope. Nope. Absolutely not. We were not having this conversation here. Not at all, actually.

"Has anyone talked to Dezi or Izaiah?" I said, cutting Matt off before he could get my name out. Trying hard not to notice the way he deflated, I turned toward the others. "It's coming down heavy out there."

Grayson's smirk turned to me as he shrugged and leaned against the counter. "I'm sure they're fine. I talked to them a couple hours ago. They should be on the road by now."

"Should we wait until they get here to pick rooms?"

"Hell no," said Grayson.

"What he means to say," said Kamille, shooting him a look, "is that we'll save them the primary and pick from everything else."

She wasted no time grabbing my hand and leading me out of the kitchen. "I know the concept of manners is hard for some people around here to grasp, but I think it goes without saying: ladies first, of course."

Trina

IT TOOK around fifteen minutes for Kamille to pull me all over the house, going from room to room in the two-story cabin. The place was gorgeous. Tall, vaulted ceilings with a mix of drywall, stone, and wood-paneled walls that cemented the modern rustic feel, especially when combined with the large stone fireplace in the center of the living room and wood ceilings that alternated throughout the entire house. It had a spacious yet cozy feel, each floor to ceiling window letting in the perfect amount of light and offering an amazing view of the snow, forest, and mountains outside. None of the public spaces felt closed in thanks to the open concept, with the kitchen, living room, and dining room all flowing together seamlessly. The owner had taken care in decorating it for the holidays, filling it with gray and white stockings over the fireplaces and multiple trees with decorations that matched the same color scheme. It was the sort of place that you came to and then never wanted to leave.

And by the end of the tour, I was even more convinced this trip was a whole ass mistake.

"Kamille," I sighed, exasperated. "I don't understand why you're so hell bent on me taking this exact room."

"Let me find out we should've picked you up some q-tips at the store so you can clean your ears."

The look I gave her made it clear I didn't find her antics cute at all.

"Fine, I'll say it again just because I love you. As perfect as this room is," she said, gesturing around the space furnished with an antique armoire, matching four-poster bed, and a sitting area with a fireplace that was a miniature version of the one downstairs, "it's nowhere near beautiful enough for me to agree to share a bathroom with that pain in the ass Grayson."

Right, because it featured a Jack and Jill bathroom with the room next door. But see, that's where her argument lost me because I didn't understand why she thought being right next to Grayson was the only option this room came with.

"So take the other room and then we can share the bathroom."

"And be close enough to hear Dezi and Izaiah bumping uglies across the hall at all hours of the night? Yeah, I'll pass on that one."

"Okaaaay." Trying to keep my irritation in check was becoming a full-time job. I was nauseous, hungry, and just wanted to lay down. "Take the room down the hall and then Grayson can have the room on the first floor."

"And let that little demon child enjoy the only room with a bit of solitude? Bitch, did you slip on a patch of ice and bump your head?" she asked, looking at me like I'd lost my mind.

"Fine. Then I'll take the room down the hall and Grayson and Matthew can take these two."

"Bestie, you're really about to give up this amazing view and the fireplace? You literally just told me it's your favorite thing about the room."

Had I said that? When was I going to learn to stop running my mouth?

I groaned, completely over this conversation and trip all together. Fine. I could deal with sharing a bathroom with Grayson. Despite his childish personality—Kamille and Deziree's words, not mine—I knew he wasn't messy. Their parents did not play that shit and we'd all been to his place enough times to know better. That left Matthew with the bedroom closest to the stairs and furthest away from me.

"Fine, fine, fine! You win, as usual." I narrowed my eyes. "You really should've gone into the corporate world. You're a shark and very persuasive when you're trying to get your way." I knew at least four people off the top of my head at my ad agency that would fold immediately under Kamille's pressure.

"I negotiate with five-year-olds all day. Your first mistake was thinking I was new to this, not true to it." She wrapped me in a hug and practically skipped out of the room as she said, "I'll have Grayson bring up your stuff so you can lay down. I know you're exhausted, boo."

Damn, did I look that bad? Shit, it didn't matter because she was right.

Giving her a quick thanks that I wasn't even sure she heard, I took one more look around before falling onto the bed. Sleep came quick, but it didn't last long before a soft knock followed by footsteps managed to pull me awake.

"Thanks, Gray. You can just sit them in the corner. I'll unpack in a little bit."

"No problem."

That's not Grayson.

My eyes popped open as I slowly sat up to find Matthew standing just inside the doorway, a smirk on his face and my two bags at his feet while his own duffle was hefted on his shoulder.

"I thought—"

"Grayson's outside trying to see if he can get hold of Izaiah. Looks like the storm's moving in faster than we thought and the snowflakes are getting thicker by the minute. Kami grabbed me instead."

"Oh."

Oh. Oh? Alone with this man for the first time in months and that was the best I could come up with?

Fucking ridiculous.

"So are you going to spend the entire trip avoiding me or…"

"Nobody's avoiding you, Matty."

Liar.

And he knew it too. But instead of calling me on it, he simply nodded his head and adjusted the bag on his shoulder. "Good. 'Cause that would be pretty hard to do since we're neighbors for the next few days."

To solidify his point, he made the journey to the bathroom door instead of the one he'd used to get into the room in the first place.

"Wait, no." I scrambled to my knees and instantly regretted the decision because why the fuck was the room spinning? Trying to get my bearings, I took a deep breath, saying, "That's Grayson's room."

He chuckled, and goddamn my raggedy ass pussy 'cause why could I hear her purring in reaction to the sound? Could he hear her too?

Had to. That was the only explanation for why his eyes were sliding over me, top to bottom, in a way I could practically feel.

"It would've been, but turns out Gray may or may not have caught Dezi and Izaiah together at the firehouse once and now he's scarred for life. He wants to be as far away from them as possible, and since Kamille made it clear him taking the room downstairs isn't an option, I offered him the room on the other side of the loft." Running his thumb across his bottom lip, he narrowed his eyes. "That's not a problem, right?"

"Of cou—" I cleared my throat since, for some reason, my voice was trying to embarrass me by going up two octaves. "No, no problem. We're friends, right?"

There was a moment—just a brief one—where it looked like he had something completely different in mind. Instead, Matt just shook his head and chuckled. "Right...friend."

And as I watched him shut the door to our shared bathroom, only one thing crossed my mind.

How the fuck am I going to take a goddamn pregnancy test with my potential baby daddy right outside the door?

matthew

WAS STARING CONSIDERED creepy because it was a hallmark of stalking or because it made people uncomfortable?

Probably the latter.

Did stalking include blowing up a person's phone multiple times over an almost two-month span even though they never answered and never called back, no matter how many messages you left?

Probably.

You'd think a nigga would catch the hint, but for once in my life, it seemed as though I was doing everything except what I was supposed to.

It'd taken twenty-six years, but I'd finally learned how to break a few rules.

"Nigga, if you stare any harder, you're gonna burn a hole in the side of her head."

I chuckled, leaning back in my chair. Maybe if I appeared relaxed, my body would do me a favor and *actually* relax. It was a great theory, but with my eyes still fastened on Trina, the tension in my shoulders—throughout my whole body, actually—didn't seem to be going anywhere.

"Is that your expert opinion or are you just guessing?"

"Expert opinion, nigga. Duh."

"And you know this because…"

"Because I can literally feel the one Kamille put in mine."

That got an even bigger laugh out of me. "Nah, pretty sure what you're feeling is the bullet she's plotting to put between your eyes if you don't leave her the fuck alone."

"Now why would I do that when fucking with her is so much fun?"

Shaking my head, I finally set my sights on Grayson, who'd taken the seat beside me. I said a silent thanks that whoever owned this place not only made sure the back porch was enclosed, but also included heating so we wouldn't freeze to death. The snow falling was finally starting to slow down, but that didn't mean it was getting any warmer. Whenever Trina and Kamille finished making their snow angels, they were going to be frozen solid.

Maybe she'll let you warm her up.

If only.

"And no matter what Kami tells y'all, she likes that shit just as much as she likes me."

"Now I know you're delusional. She can't stand your ass."

He waved me off as if what I'd said was inconsequential.

"That's just what she wants you to think. We know the truth."

I just shook my head. Suddenly, laughter filled the air, and my eyes immediately tracked the sound back to the source. It wasn't the same high-pitched giggle from my memories, but it affected me all the same.

With her head tossed back and a smile on her face as she tried to dodge the snow Kamille was throwing at her, Trina looked completely carefree. It was certainly different from how she'd looked on the way up here. The complete opposite of how she'd looked when she found out I'd be staying in the room next to hers.

Was it my presence that was fucking with her or did something else have her stressed? The simplest thing to do would've been to ask, but would she be honest?

Probably not. At least not with me. Not anymore.

"Does my sister know you're fucking on her best friend?"

Snapping my head in Gray's direction, I couldn't help but feel slightly nervous. For someone who always appeared to be on joke time, he sure knew how to shift the mood. And apparently he was a lot more intuitive than we ever gave him credit for. His expression didn't suggest he wanted to fuck me up, but looks could be deceiving.

"Gray…"

"It's a simple question, Matt. One you had to know would come up since you literally can't take your eyes off Trina. You're not even trying to hide it."

"What's your point?" I asked. No, actually it was more of a grunt.

"My point is, your ex-girlfriend might be wrapped up in my best friend at the moment, but she's not oblivious. If and when they eventually make it up here, she's going to notice the lovesick puppy act you've got going on here. And she's going to have some questions, so I'm gonna ask you again just to give you a little practice—does Dezi know you're messing around with one of her best friends?"

I thought about denying it. Almost did, but what was the point? I wouldn't be able to convince Trina to give this—give us—a try if I couldn't even admit that there was something here worth trying. Might as well start now.

"Nah, she doesn't know. No one does." I gave his question a second thought. "And we're not messing around." Not currently anyway. "It only happened once."

Technically that wasn't true since it happened multiple times over a single weekend, but those were semantics.

"Once...and she's got you pressed like this?" Grayson shook his head as he stood, hand coming down on my shoulder. "Must've been some night."

I didn't say anything for a few moments, not expecting him to be finished. When it was clear he was, I asked, "That's all you have to say? Nothing about how fucked up being with Trina is or how you should beat my ass for doing some shit like this to Dezi?"

He let out a snort. "I mean, I can offer to beat your ass if you really want me to, but we both know Dezi's capable of doing that all on her own."

He had a point there.

"And yeah, it might not be the most ideal setup, but don't people always say you can't help who you're attracted to? Y'all are both adults, so unless you suddenly decided to start being a piece of shit in the last few months, I'm going to assume whatever happened between the two of you was consensual."

"Of course it was."

"A'ight, so then what exactly am I supposed to do? I'm the last nigga to tell you who you should and shouldn't be fucking." His eyes drifted in the direction of the two women who were finally headed inside, making their way through the door that led to the mud room. Was he watching Trina or Kamille? I had my own suspicions, but kept them to myself.

"What I will say is, I suggest you figure your shit out before something happens and life figures it out for you."

Not waiting for me to respond, Grayson made his way back in the house—presumably to check on the chili he'd started—leaving me to my own thoughts.

"I can't believe of all the things you could've done for your birthday, you came out with little ole me, Matty," Trina giggled.

She never giggled. Not this high-pitched one anyway, but considering the number of tequila shots we'd taken at the first bar and then the second, it was obvious she was starting to feel them. Shit, so was I. But those giggles...they didn't sound out of place coming from her. They sounded sexy as fuck.

Just like her.

With her locs pulled back in a high ponytail, the oversized button-up that barely hit her mid-thigh, calf-high socks, and ankle boots she had on, there was no other way to describe her.

"Where else would I be, Tini?" My body closed in around hers as the elevator passed floor after floor.

"Uh-uh, don't say it like that. The only reason you're even here is because you had to come for work."

The way she was staring up at me put the rest of the world out of focus. Not that I minded.

"That might be what brought me here, but it's not why I stayed." *That work trip ended three days ago.*

As if they had a mind of their own, my fingers reached out, tracing along her chin. Her hazelnut skin was glowing. Maybe it was the low lighting of the elevator or maybe it was the alcohol. Either way, she looked...fuck.

Whatever it was pulled me in closer. Close enough to hear her breath catch in her throat.

"So why'd you stay?"

That was the question, wasn't it?

The easy answer was because we were friends. Had been since she'd first moved to the neighborhood when we were kids. You were supposed to spend your birthday with friends, weren't you? Pretty sure you weren't supposed to kiss them, though.

So when and why had I made the decision to do exactly that?

My lips pressed lightly against hers as my hand cupped her chin, shoulder lifting as I leaned into her even further. She tasted like...peaches and cinnamon. There was a hint of tequila there too, but as she opened for me and my tongue caressed hers, the flavor immediately evoked the image of the cobbler we'd had for dessert at the soul food restaurant.

And I wanted more.

❄

AND MORE WAS WHAT I GOT.

More kisses.

More touching.

A hell of a lot more skin.

The problem with getting more, especially for a short amount of time, was that it never seemed to be enough.

Trina

"TOMORROW? What do you mean they're not getting here until tomorrow?" Kamille whined on the other side of the bathroom door, where I assumed she was getting dressed now that she was fresh out the shower after our snow angel escapade.

"I'm just telling you what Grayson said. We beat most of the storm by leaving early and they pretty much got trapped in it. They only made it about halfway up before the roads became impassable. It wouldn't be safe for them to keep trying, so they found a lodge that still had a few rooms available and they're going to stay there until crews can clear a path up the mountain. Right now, they're thinking they should be here by tomorrow night as long as the weather doesn't get any worse."

I had a sneaking suspicion that was just wishful thinking and it'd take an extra day, which meant the four of us were on our own.

Did I say four?

The two lines looking back at me from both pregnancy tests on the sink said that count might not be accurate.

"Please say sike."

Apparently what was meant to be an inside thought was a very loud outside one.

"Are you in there talking to yourself?" Kamille called through the door.

This girl. "Ma'am, why are you all in my business?" I managed to say back.

"Because you're in *my* bathroom."

Right. Suddenly I was rethinking my brilliant plan to do this here. But it seemed better than the alternative of doing it in the one I was currently sharing with my baby daddy. And since he was using ours and I was eager to get this over with...

Now I was wishing I'd just ignored the problem all weekend and waited until I got home. And despite the fact that overpowering nausea was what had driven me to take the tests in the first place, the wave that was hitting me now had little to do with the confirmed ball of cells itself and everything to do with reality closing in around me.

Something between a very deranged laugh and a sob escaped me.

A goddamn baby? Had we fucked on every available inch of his hotel suite that weekend? Yeah, okay, sure. And it's not like I was one of those girls who couldn't put two and two together that sex could always result in a baby, but weren't condoms supposed to guard against that? And I knew for a fact we'd used them because I hadn't gotten a chance to refill my birth control that week, so I'd been adamant about having them. We used a condom every single—

Shit.

Every time except the last time.

✳

"What happened to letting me shower alone?" I asked, not bothering to turn around. The creak of the bathroom door clued me into his presence, so the cool air caressing my skin from the open glass shower door wasn't a surprise. Neither was the feel of his arms wrapping around my thick waist.

What was surprising was how natural this all felt. As if Matt and I had been doing this a lot longer than a matter of days. We'd known each other for years—over a decade, actually—but if someone had said to me at the top of the year that the prospect of seeing him, touching him, hearing him laugh with that deep yet soft voice of his would send the butterflies in my stomach into a frenzy, I would've called bullshit immediately.

*He may have been one of my closest friends, but he'd also been **with** one of my closest friends for so long that this never even seemed like an option.*

Now ten-year-old me?

She would've been giddy at the thought that her schoolgirl crush was being fully realized. Long before any of us were even thinking about what a boyfriend or girlfriend was, just one look from Matty made me blush, but those feelings disappeared around the time we hit our final year of middle school.

I'd been happier than anyone when he and Dezi finally got together senior year of college after months of stolen looks and constant flirtations.

So how was it that six months after they'd broken up, my crush started rearing its head again? Right around the time he was put on a project that required him to be in New York for weeks at a time.

A project that was officially done as of a few days ago.

The trail of kisses he began placing on my shoulder pulled me from my thoughts before I could dwell on the fact that he'd be leaving soon. Before I could remember that I had no idea when I'd see him again or what our relationship would be like once we did.

I turned around, those eyes that almost seemed to see right through me catching mine.

Could we go back to just being friends now that I knew what it was like to have his goatee tickle my skin as he kissed me with those full lips? Or now that I knew how it felt when his eyes locked in on my every movement, listening intently to every word, anticipating every need, making me feel as though I was the only woman in the room?

How could I look him in the eye and act as if I hadn't experienced the way his dick stretched me so perfectly, providing a sense of fullness I'd never had before?

Like right now.

"Fuck, Matty," I moaned, dropping the washcloth so I could wrap my arms around his neck, my hand instantly grabbing the back of his head. His hands gripped the back of my thighs as he held me up effortlessly.

Pressing his forehead to mine, he said, "I missed you."

The words were followed by a thrust so deep, I swear I could feel it in my chest.

"It was...only...ten min—" My eyes and head rolled back at the same time as his head dipped down, taking one of my nipples between his lips.

What was I saying?

"Ten minutes too long, Tini."

And he proved it by stroking me until I came all over his dick not once but twice, even though he'd already pulled several out of me that morning.

I couldn't tell you which way was up by the time ropes of his cum began to coat my walls, triggering another mini orgasm. But what was obvious was the look of pure concentration and adoration on his face.

So obvious that my heart skipped a beat.

"BITCH, WHY DON'T I HEAR ANY WA—"

Kamille came barreling through the door, jolting me out of my stupor. I waited for the end of her question but it never came. She was too busy staring down at the evidence left on the sink.

"Friend, I think you might've smacked me a little too hard with one of those snowballs. 'Cause I know my optometrist didn't lie when she told me I had twenty-twenty vision."

The weak laugh that left me was almost involuntary. "If that's the case, we must've given each other matching concussions 'cause I see them too."

"Tiniiiiii." The way she dragged my nickname out was almost comical when you paired it with her wide-eyed stare. "You been letting a nigga shoot up the club? I'm shocked, appalled, and proud all at once."

My wince was automatic.

"You may only be appalled once you find out the who." The weight of the secret had been draining me for weeks. I needed to let it out to someone.

I stood, needing to get out of the bathroom and away from the evidence. Keeping the towel wrapped tightly around me, I plopped down on the bench at the end of the bed.

"Please don't tell me it's the guy on your team you said looked like Chewbacca. My stomach is turning at the thought."

That would make this a lot easier, actually.

"No. Think gorgeous, strong-jawed, sweet and silent lawyer type who's closer to home." A lot closer. I stared at my hands. "Like in this house close."

The silence that followed was deafening. Shit, did she pass out? One glance up and it was clear that no, Kamille was still very much upright, but there was no telling for how long since I was pretty sure she wasn't breathing.

"Kamille."

No response.

"Kamille, say something!"

"My bad, girl. I must've blacked out for a second 'cause I know you didn't just say that Matthew is the nigga you've been riding from here to kingdom come."

Dropping my head into my hands, I groaned, completely mortified. "Kami, please."

"Uh-uh, don't *Kami, please* me! When? Where? How?" She paused. "Actually, don't elaborate on that last one. I know how bouncing on a dick works. I'm quite good at it myself. Just maybe not 'have a baby by me, baby' good."

If looks could kill, she'd be in the grave. "You're not cute."

"The lie detector says that is a lie, beloved."

Sitting down next to me, she didn't say another word, waiting for me to answer the questions she'd already laid out on the table.

"You know Matt's firm put him on their expansion project for the clients relocating to New York."

It wasn't a secret. It had come up in conversation plenty of times in the group. Especially because every time he came, he made it a point to see me, just like I'd done the few times I'd gone to Cali for a project or meeting. Dezi did it all the time with both of us when she traveled for work too.

"Right, the project's been going on for the better part of a year."

I gave her a nod. "And the last week of the project also happened to be the week of his birthday." Which was something she also already knew. "I guess we got a lot closer over that time than we thought."

Phone calls at all hours. Inside jokes. Syncing up our schedules whenever he was coming into town. Dinner. Coffee. Lunch. Movies. Chilling at my condo or his hotel room. It all felt so innocent in the moment. Like two friends reconnecting—or rather connecting in a way we hadn't ever done before since so much of our dynamic was created by being a group of four. But with that four broken down to just us two...something developed that I don't think either of us anticipated.

I said as much to Kamille.

"Well damn, Trina. I wasn't excepting you to say all that. I thought it was just as simple as you wanting to sample the dick. You know that man is bowlegged as fuck."

A laugh bubbled up from my chest and once it started, there was no stopping it. She joined in, both of us nearly falling back as we tried to pull ourselves together.

Once we finally managed some semblance of control, she asked one of the questions I'd been dreading. "Okay, so y'all were basically dating without even realizing it, shit got physical, and now Aunt Flo has skipped town like the raggedy heffa she is. And really, all of this would be inconsequential if we weren't talking about Matty here, but we are." She paused. "Be honest, bestie. Are you in love with him?"

Was I?

I'd been trying to sort through my feelings ever since that night, but the answer seemed too scary to acknowledge or admit. If I was, did it make the prospect of this relationship—*this baby*—any easier? Scarier? Any less far-fetched?

"Maybe." That was the best I could give her. The fact that the line between lover and friend could be so thin had never occurred to me, but now that it was a reality, it was hard to know how to process it. I'd always wanted to be a mom, but this wasn't exactly how I'd envisioned embarking on the journey.

But who better to do it with than a man you know you can call one of your closest friends?

"You know you have to tell Dezireé, right? Even if you decide not to keep the baby."

I did.

"How are you going to tell her?"

"Shit, I have no idea. Maybe we should check with Siri. Something like, 'how do you ask your bestie to be your baby's godmother when she's already fucked your baby daddy?'"

I laughed, trying to make light of the situation, but stopped as soon as it became clear that Kamille wasn't laughing with me. She was too busy staring at something—*someone*—at the door.

Nerves instantly flooded my system. "Please tell me she's not miraculously standing behind me."

"No..." she said, letting the word drop off as her eyes stayed locked on their target.

"But it seems like the baby daddy in question might be," Matthew said, filling the room with an eerie calm only he could create.

Fuck. Me.

matthew

I WAS SUPPOSED to be delivering a message. Something about dinner being ready.

It was hard to remember with the new set of words leaving my mouth.

"But it seems like the baby daddy in question might be."

They were such a jumbled mess in my mind that I still wasn't sure how I managed to get them out, considering it felt as though the world had been pulled right out from under me.

Could anyone else feel it?

Probably not, since Kamille had no problem finding her footing as she stood and made her escape out the door, saying something about making sure Grayson hadn't fucked up the firehouse specialty. At least that's what I thought she'd said. For all I knew, she could've been reciting nursery rhymes and I wouldn't be able to tell the difference.

Baby.

Baby.

Baby.

A fucking baby.

"Matty…"

The sound of her voice snapping me back to reality was a testament to just how much of a hold Trina had on me. Her face came into focus as I took a few steps into the room. Which was the wrong move, based on the way she instantly stood and pushed past me out the door.

"Trina."

If I didn't know any better, I would've thought her name had been an inside thought because she didn't break her stride. Just continued making her way down the short hallway toward the back stairwell that led to the second floor landing.

"Trina!" I said, the bass and volume of my voice becoming more insistent.

"Shhhh!" she hissed, whipping around halfway up the stairs as she clutched her towel tight to her body. "You are loud as hell right now."

"Then stop ignoring me."

"I'm not ignoring you. I just…" She paused to take a breath. "I would rather not have this conversation in my towel in the middle of Kamille's room—or in the hallway, for that matter."

"Cool," I said with a nod, moving toward her until only one step separated us.

"What are you doing?"

"You don't want to have this conversation out here. That's fine. We'll have it upstairs in your room. Or mine. Take your pick 'cause it really doesn't matter to me. The point is we're having the conversation."

"Now?"

"Right now."

My tone left no room for discussion. When she realized she was fighting a losing battle, she turned and led the way upstairs. What felt like a year's time to get to the room was actually less than a minute. Once we were safely behind her bedroom door, I wasted no time getting straight to the point.

"You're pregnant?"

Instead of moving to the other side of the room like I thought she would, she held her ground just a few steps from me. "According to the two pregnancy tests I just took in Kamille's bathroom, yes."

There was no need to ask who she thought the father was. I'd heard that part loud and clear and I knew better than probably anyone how lackluster her dating life had been over the last year. We'd talked about it enough times.

"But how?" I knew the when. We'd only been together that way for one weekend. A weekend I couldn't get out of my mind if I tried. Not that I had—tried, that is.

I'd been too busy replaying it over and over again, fucking my hand so intensely to the images my mind conjured that I was always left breathless with cum covering my hand and stomach.

"The shower."

Two words. That was all it took to transport me back to the exact moment she was referring to.

The email confirming my flight to San Francisco had just come through. And despite Trina only being a few feet away in the bathroom, that confirmation had me feeling like she was a million miles away.

Call it desperation, need, infatuation or whatever you want, but something led me into that shower with her, needing to touch her, feel her, *be* with her in whatever way possible. I couldn't express what I was feeling with words, but our bodies had done the talking for us for two days. Why not one more time?

And now I was realizing just how reckless I'd been.

But...even as I silently chastised myself for the slip-up, I didn't feel an ounce of regret.

"Shit."

"Yeah, exactly."

We stood there in silence for a while, neither of us able to say a damn thing.

That wasn't entirely true.

There were words I wanted to say, but I wasn't sure if she was ready to hear them.

"I don't know what I want to do yet," she said as if she needed to get that out of the way. Did she think I expected her to have all the answers right now? Because I didn't.

"Okay."

"I need to think, but right now everything is just a shitty, jumbled mess, so if you're going to want to go into lawyer mode and argue about keeping this baby or not, it's not happening."

"Okay."

"O...kay?" I watched as her expression morphed from one of confusion to exasperation. "*Okay?* That's all you have to say? Matt, you act like I just told your ass I want butter pecan ice cream, not chocolate. Don't you think finding out I'm pregnant warrants a little more than just 'okay'?"

Closing the distance between us, I wrapped an arm around her waist in an attempt to pull her to me, but she tried—and failed—to step out of reach. Instead, it made me move in even closer. We kept up that little dance until bumping into the bed left her with nowhere to go.

"Fine. Tell me what you want to hear, Trina. You want me to apologize for being so reckless with your body in that moment when going without a condom wasn't something we talked about beforehand? I'm deeply sorry for that."

And I was, but fuck, her walls felt so goddamn amazing pulsing around me with nothing between us that my only regret was the carelessness of it, not the moment itself.

"Should I say sorry you've been dealing with this possibility on your own and the fact you thought you couldn't come to me with this? Because I'm sorry for that too. I apologize that I didn't try harder to get you to answer my phone calls or text messages. That I didn't get my ass on a plane, a train, or in a damn car and make my way to you so we could sit and talk about what happened between us and how we feel about each other."

Her brow furrowed in frustration as if I still weren't saying the right things.

"None of that was what you wanted to hear? Fine, what about this: I'm here. No matter what you decide to do, regardless of how you want to handle this, I'm here.

"You want to keep the baby? Just let me know and I'll start working on a registry and baby names right now while you make your first doctor's appointment. You want to have an abortion? I'll go with you to the consultation and appointment and hold your hand during the entire thing. I'll take you home once it's over and lay with you, binge watch your favorite reality shows, order from your favorite Korean spot, and get you whatever you need until you feel better. Tell me what it is you want to do and I'm right there, ready and waiting with you to do it."

"That's no—" She shook her head, her frustration and confusion only growing as she sat on the edge of the bed. "That's not what—"

It was almost like the words were caught in her throat. Like she couldn't get them out, which was fine because I knew where she was headed. Could see the path she was going down.

I dropped into a crouch, needing her to look at me—to really hear me. "Tini, I swear on everything, I will give you almost anything you want, right here and right now. But what I'm not about to do is apologize because the weekend happened.

"I'm not sorry about the nights we spent stuffing our faces with kimchi and bao buns. Definitely not sorry for all the times we fell asleep watching whatever true crime documentary you talked me into even though that shit creeps me the fuck out. I'm not sorry for every moment I've spent dreaming about you or how it felt to wake up with you wrapped in my arms. And I'm damn sure not apologizing for getting the chance to experience what it was like to have you come apart on my dick over and over again in that hotel room. If anything, I'm just sorry it took us so long to get there."

"How can you say that?"

"How can you imply anything different?" I shot back.

"You and Dezi—"

"Had been broken up for over a year when we had sex, Trina. And drifted apart long before that."

"It doesn't matter. You were still her boyfriend!"

"Not at the time!"

"Semantics!"

"Nah, an important distinction, actually. One I need you to get through that stubborn head of yours so you can stop acting like we did something wrong when we both know we didn't."

I placed a finger under her chin to keep her from breaking eye contact. "And stop acting as if I'm some piece of property that you stole and not an adult who made a choice to be with someone I wanted. You didn't trick me. You didn't seduce me, and you didn't take me from her. Saying anything otherwise isn't just insulting to me, it insults you and the relationship Dezi has with Izaiah too."

Should I have been upfront with Dezireé when I realized I was developing feelings for Trina? Yeah, if for no other reason than to give her the courtesy and respect she deserved. I would need to rectify that immediately. Especially now because no matter what decision she came to about this pregnancy, I had every intention of pursuing a relationship with Trina.

Between one beat and the next, I watched as her shoulders dropped, the tension finally leaving them. "All that guilt you're carrying, mama? You gotta let that shit go. Is that why you've been avoiding me?"

Trina nodded and her eyes began to well with tears. "I didn't know how to look at you—how to talk to you—and reconcile how you make me feel with who we are to each other. Who we are to Dezi."

"And I understand that, but you're not the only one who was left confused by that weekend. Shit, I still don't have the words to fully describe it. All I know is leading up to that night in the elevator, every time I looked at you, my heart stuttered. And every time I had to leave New York to head back home, it got harder and harder to be away from you."

Leaning in, I touched my forehead to hers. "And it's so fucking hard being in this house with you and not being able to touch you the way I want. To feel you the way I *need* to."

My knees hit the floor as one hand drifted toward the towel she was still clutching. Using my free hand, I gripped the back of her head, taking her lips in a soft yet urgent kiss.

A whimper escaped her, and for a second, I got the impression she wasn't going to kiss me back. Just before the doubt could creep in, her lips parted, welcoming my tongue with hers. With her distracted, it took nothing to pull the towel from her grasp and let it fall open.

"Matty," she gasped as I pulled away, leaning down to take a nipple into my mouth. The moan that followed as my teeth scraped along the hardening bud instantly made my dick hard.

I continued, giving the same amount of attention to its twin, even as her body fell completely back on the comforter.

"What are you doing?" Her words were a whisper, but the moan she let out as my mouth followed the lines of her body until I had one leg angled flat on the bed and the other over my shoulder was louder.

A lot louder.

"Reminding you of how good we could be if you give us another chance." I nipped at the inside of her thigh with my teeth. "And showing you just how much I missed you."

Trina

YES, *yes, yes.*

Wait, no. No, no, no, no.

Fuck, I couldn't make up my mind. How was my brain supposed to come up with a reasonable ass thought when Matty's head was between my thighs and his lips were wrapped around my clit? The man was worshiping me like he'd found the fountain of youth down there. Shit, with how wet I was, he might damn well have.

After one particular leg-shaking swipe of his tongue, I committed to the thought that this was a great idea. As he pushed two fingers into me, pumping them in and out at a steady pace, I amended my previous thought.

This is actually the best idea possible.

Was the world spinning or just me?

"You taste so fucking good, mama." His words came out as a groan, mixing their way into the sound of him devouring me. A sound that not only seemed to bounce off the walls of the room, but was so all-around filthy that I couldn't help but whimper as my thighs tightened around his head like his own personal pair of earmuffs. As I hurtled straight toward an orgasm, he went even harder as if he really did have a point to prove.

Maybe he did.

Whatever it was, I might have to have him explain it to me again if it got me a repeat performance.

With every twirl of his tongue, my moans grew louder. Bolder.

Christ, can Kamille and Grayson hear me right now? I hope—

Cries filled with the word 'yes' broke free from my throat, stopping the thought in its tracks. Almost immediately, the groan Matt let loose as I came on his tongue rivaled my own.

The real question should've been could they hear *us*? No matter what the answer was, I decided I didn't give a damn. Not when the sounds of his appreciation made my pussy wetter by the second.

"Fuck, I missed this. Did you miss it, mama?"

Did I miss this? Of course I had. Somehow I'd developed a craving for something I was never supposed to have in the first place, and now that I was getting my first real fix in months, it was damn near making me feel like a fiend.

And I tried my hardest to explain it to him, but I couldn't seem to form the words.

It was too damn hard to focus when I could taste myself on his tongue. When his hands were skimming over every stretch mark, every roll, every inch of skin he could find like he couldn't get his fill.

"I asked you a question, Tini."

"Matty." Maybe I should've been ashamed of the whine in my voice, but I couldn't bring myself to be.

"I'm serious. Tell me you miss this." He kissed me again, this time sucking on my tongue in a way that had me reaching between us to push down the sweatpants he'd changed into at some point after we'd gotten in the house. "Tell me you miss me."

"I missed you, baby." The words came out in a gasp as I took the initiative to line his thick shaft up with my entrance. All he wanted to do was talk and what I needed was to *feel* him. The anticipation alone was enough to kill me. And maybe it did because as soon as he thrust into me, my entire body shuddered while his moans drowned out my own. "I missed you so fucking much."

"And that's why ignoring this isn't an option anymore, mama." Our eyes met and—fuck, why did it feel like he was staring straight into the heart of me?

Was he right? Did I need to just stop fighting this, stop avoiding him, and just…give us both a chance to be happy?

I could go into deep thought debating the intricacies of our feelings or the situation. Ruminate about what it would be like if we decided to move forward and I let go of the guilt or stress or whatever the fuck else was holding me back.

I could do all of that.

But at the moment, the only thing I wanted to think about was how good it felt for Matty to be fucking me again. The way he was trying his hardest to keep eye contact, but every time my walls pulsed around him, those beautiful eyes of his threatened to roll into the back of his head…

It was such a turn-on.

So much so that with each stroke he delivered, I made sure to tighten them, knowing that each time brought him closer to being undone.

"Shit, Tini. What the fuck are you trying to do to me?"

Running my hand across his cheek as I arched my back, another moan falling from my lips, I somehow managed to say, "You feel so good, Matty."

Placing my legs completely on his shoulders, he leaned in, each thrust more punishing than the last. I could feel every inch of him and every keening cry let him know it. He was so goddamn deep, the stretch and burn perfect in every way.

"Tell me you want this cum as much as you wanted this dick, mama."

All I managed was a whimper as he kissed me hungrily.

"You gonna make me repeat myself, Tini?"

"I—" A sob broke free. "I want it."

"You telling me I can paint these walls?"

Could he? Shit, even if I wasn't pregnant, did he really think I'd be telling him no? Not fucking likely, considering all it would take was a few more thrusts and I'd be falling right over the edge of the cliff.

My entire body was vibrating, each of my senses on high alert.

"Please. *Pleeease.*" And because he knew I was begging not just for his cum but my own release as well, those talented fingers of his slipped between us, playing with my clit without missing a beat.

Snapping my eyes shut, his name fell from my lips in a chant as I came all over his dick, my pussy milking him for the prize he promised me.

Matty spilled his warm cum inside of me, mixing it with my own, and I swear to god, my pussy purred in reaction as he collapsed, careful not to put his full weight on me.

Did we lay there for two minutes? Five? Ten? Thirty? I had no fucking clue. The only thing that registered was the soft kisses Matt placed on my eyes, cheeks, and lips before wrapping me in his arms.

"I think we made a mess," he whispered against my skin.

Giggling, I shook my head and snuggled closer. "No, you made a mess. I was just an innocent bystander."

"Sure you were."

Somehow we managed not to fall asleep. Or really, he didn't. I was happily drifting off, vaguely aware of him leaving the bed and coming back with what felt like a warm washcloth to clean me up. As exhausted as my body felt, I was also starving, which was why I resisted protesting when he pulled my pajamas from my bag and helped me into the shower and then get dressed.

"Do you want me to meet you downstairs, or do you want to lay here and catch a nap while I hop in the shower to clean up your" —I cut him a look—"our mess?"

"I'll wait," I said, even though my stomach was literally screaming at me to do the opposite.

"No running away?"

On the surface, it was a simple question, but the nervous energy radiating off him let me know it was anything but.

"No running."

And I was going to try to stick to that promise for as long as I possibly could.

| SATURDAY |

JASMINE.

The scent wrapped around me like a warm blanket. One that triggered a sense of déjà vu, taking me back to another weekend in a very different bed, but a similar circumstance.

My eyes opened, fighting against the near-blinding sunlight peeking through the windows, and searched for the source. I didn't have to look far since it was coming from the gorgeous woman currently cuddled into my chest, seemingly right at home positioned on top of my arm. No wonder the shit felt so stiff. Considering a half-dressed Trina was the cause, though, there was no way in hell I was about to complain. Not when I'd spent the last couple of months dreaming about waking up to this very sight.

Sitting up as carefully as possible, I did the best I could not to wake her. With the way we'd worn each other out before and after dinner, Trina could use all the rest she could get. Well, that and she tended to be cranky as hell when she first woke up, no matter what time it was. I'd figured that out during our plentiful

—but platonic—overnight sleepovers during those New York trips.

My eyes traced over every line of her face, taking her in.

Those full lips, pulled into a perfect pout.

The adorable slight scrunch of her nose. Not the type that appeared in reaction to a nightmare, but more like she was fighting the urge to wake up.

The bonnet I'd slipped onto her head to keep her locs fresh and secured right after she fell asleep.

Moving lower, my eyes snagged on the way her right hand was splayed across her stomach, almost as if she were cradling it.

Was that a coincidence or her subconscious reminding her of yesterday's test results? I wasn't sure, but the shit hit me in the chest anyway.

"Staring at me when you could be closing those blinds so we can both go back to sleep? I don't know whether to be flattered, creeped out, or just very annoyed."

Maybe I should've been embarrassed that she'd caught me watching her, but I wasn't. Not in the least bit. If you could find me a nigga who didn't get caught up in his woman's beauty first thing in the morning, you can best believe you've found a nigga who ain't worth shit.

And it was clear that she didn't really mind, based on the smirk fighting to take over her face. So instead of ducking my head and shying away, I just gave her a smile of my own.

"How you expect me to get my ass up and do anything when you're holding me hostage?" I nodded my head toward the arm still trapped underneath her. "Shit, if you want to be for real, I was sitting here trying to figure out how to chew the damn thing off so I could escape."

"Oh, really?" she said, pulling away and freeing the arm in question. "Well, what if I said you and your smart ass mouth could get out, then?" The little mean act she was trying to put on wasn't fooling anybody. That twinkle in her sleepy gaze overshadowed it by a mile.

"Then I'd have to remind you that we fell asleep in my room last night, not yours." Something I hadn't expected initially. Even after the way she'd come apart on my dick and kept shooting me looks while we devoured the chili as we watched *Christmas with the Kranks* with Kamille and Grayson, I'd thought she'd want her space. The creaking of the bathroom door and the mattress shifting might have jolted me awake, but it was the sight of her in my bed, lip pulled between her teeth as she leaned up for a kiss that really caught me off guard.

But like I said earlier, complaining was nowhere on my agenda.

"Fine, then I'll leave."

Just as quick as she called herself trying to get out of bed, I shifted our bodies until she was right under me. "Now who said you could do that, Tini?"

"Pretty sure I don't need your permission, Matty."

"Yeah, well," I said, using one hand to brush away a stray loc that had fallen from her bonnet. "I'm not quite ready to let you go yet."

Between one breath and the next, my lips were pressed to hers. Maybe we didn't even need to get out of bed today. Shit was perfect just the way it was.

"Mmmm, but you can't keep me trapped here forever."

"And why not?"

"Well, first of all," she said with a giggle, "as much as I enjoy kissing you, morning breath is a real thing."

"Damn, break my heart, why don't you?"

"Awww." She leaned up for another quick kiss. "And two, I seem to recall something about a promise to build a snowman with me today."

With a groan, I moved to sit up, helping her to do the same as I did. "Oh, right. That."

"Yeah, that," she giggled.

As much as I wanted to, I didn't protest when she stood and stretched, clearly hell bent on getting the day started. A quick gaze at the clock told me it was noon, which meant we'd actually managed to sleep in a few hours.

"Meet back here in an hour?" I asked, standing myself.

"Definitely not." Her knowing gaze met my confused one. "We both know if I bring my ass back in this room, fully dressed or not, we won't be making snowmen. More like angels in the sheets."

I mean, shit, was it my fault she was so damn irresistible?

Clutching my chest, I attempted—and probably failed—to look hurt. "Don't act like I'm some heathen with no home training."

"I would never insult your mama like that!" Her head tilted a bit as if she was considering something. "But I do think you forgot how you were raised somewhere along the way."

Someone was full of jokes. But if she was playing around, it meant that some of the heaviness that had been weighing on her had disappeared, and I was grateful for that.

"Don't act like you wouldn't enjoy whatever alternative I could come up with."

Trina's lack of a response told me she knew I was right. But instead of pushing my luck, I just pushed her toward the bathroom door.

"Go ahead, I'll meet you downstairs. Coffee and muffins will be ready and waiting, I promise."

It only took me forty-five minutes to get myself together. By the time I made it downstairs, I was surprised to see that both Kamille and Grayson were nowhere to be found. Grayson might not be an early bird, but Kami usually was.

"Kami, you good in there?" I asked, knocking lightly on her door.

After a bit of shuffling and a muffled yelp, she opened the door looking...nervous? Anxious? I couldn't put my finger on it, but whatever it was, she was trying her hardest to ensure I couldn't see into her room.

"Hey...everything okay?"

"Uhhh, y-yeah, I'm good." The smile plastered on her face was fake, but I decided not to push her on it. "Everything okay with you and Trina? I mean about...you know."

Yeah, I did. "I think so. I mean, it seems to be, so we're just going to go with it for now and hope for the best." Clearing my throat because talking about this with her when the other member of their trio didn't know felt like I was breaking yet another unspoken rule, I quickly switched subjects.

"I'm finna make us some coffee and warm up some of the muffins we picked up yesterday before Trina and I head out. She wants to play in the snow." I chuckled at that last part because it made her sound like the big little kid she was. "Want to join us?"

Before Kamille could answer, something shifted behind her. Even with her trying to cover it with the loudest fake yawn I'd ever witnessed, I could still tell something was up.

"I'm okay, I think I'm just going to chill in the house. That snow took a lot out of me yesterday. And I was up late baking cookies and whatnot."

No wonder the faint scent of gingerbread was flowing through the house.

"Besides, I think the two of you could use some alone time." A genuine smile crossed her face. "I'll catch up with you a little later."

"A'ight, bet."

Trying not to take it too personally when she quickly closed the door in my face, I turned and made my way toward the kitchen. No point in asking Grayson. I already knew his answer was going to be a hell no.

The coffee and muffins were ready and waiting for Trina by the time she made her way downstairs.

"Looks like it's just us. Kamille turned down my offer."

"Yeah, I checked in on Grayson, but he didn't answer when I knocked."

Apparently she had the same thought I did earlier about him sleeping even later than us, but after that weird interaction with Kamille, suddenly I wasn't so sure.

"I checked in on Dezi too," she said, looking sheepish.

"They okay?"

"Yeah, the snow stopped wherever they are too, so they're hoping to be able to either get up here tonight or early in the morning."

Which meant the little bubble we'd managed to scrape together since last night just might get burst sooner rather than later.

"Guess we better eat up and head out, then."

THIS SHIT WAS PITIFUL. My snowman-making abilities had seriously gone downhill since the last time I'd done this ten years ago. I couldn't even blame it on being twenty-six because Trina's looked fucking immaculate. Now I understood why she'd told me no when I'd offered to help with hers instead of making my own.

"Your snowbaby is really about to be out here naked in the cold." She shook her head. "I should call the people on you for being so neglectful. Like a scarf and hat are literally the bare minimum."

"He's made of snow! Why would I bring that shit to keep him warm?" I laughed.

"Because Frosty set the standard and you're falling woefully below it." She balled her lips up in fake disgust as she went back to fixing the hat on her own creation's head. "You really got me concerned 'cause what if you forget to put a hat on our baby's head?"

Now I was smiling for a different reason. She was thinking about our future and it had me feeling fucking giddy.

"I know better than that."

"Yeah, you better."

After a few beats of silence, she turned to look at me, worry written on her face.

"How are we going to do this?" she asked in a faint voice, wrapping her arms around her middle. It may have been freezing outside, but I knew the gesture had nothing to do with the temperature.

I stood, dusting the snow from my hands. "And when you say this, you mean…"

"Take your pick. Telling Deziree. Deciding whether or not to keep the baby. And if I do decide I want to keep it, you literally live across the country. There aren't enough frequent flyer miles in the world to make flying back and forth that much make sense."

Taking the few steps it took to close the gap, I reached out and gripped the edge of her sleeve, pulling her in until she was securely in my arms and she'd wrapped hers around my neck.

"You're right. Hopping on a flight every time you have a doctor's appointment or an ice cream craving probably isn't the most feasible way to approach our situation." A moment of hurt flickered across her face and I could already feel her trying to pull away. "Which is why it's perfect luck that the firm planned on relocating me to the city after the holidays."

She froze. "Which city?"

I chuckled. "The same city where my very gorgeous friend who happens to be carrying my child lives."

"You're joking."

"Nah. Turns out I did such a good job handling the client moves and whatnot that a few of them requested I be put on local retainer on a more permanent basis."

When the partners first called me in to tell me the news, I couldn't believe my luck. Truth be told, as much as I enjoyed living in California, I missed the East Coast. Missed being close to home and everyone there. But more than any of that, every time I had to get on a plane and leave Trina behind, it got harder and harder. Especially after that weekend. New York might not be Oakwood, but it had everything I needed.

And now with this…situation, seemed to me the universe was trying to tell me something and was over me not taking the hint.

The smack Trina delivered to the back of my head wasn't the reaction I was expecting. "Why didn't you say anything?"

"Ouch! When was I supposed to do that, Tini? When you were ignoring all of my attempts to reach out to you or while you were ignoring me on the ride up here?"

Her look turned sheepish. "Fine, I'll let you have that one."

"How gracious," I snickered.

"Seriously, Trina. I meant what I said yesterday. My plan is to be there no matter what you choose to do because at the end of the day, this"—I gestured between the two of us—"is something I'm ready and willing to put in work for. And nothing is going to scare me away."

"It sounds good…"

"But…"

"But there's still the question of how do we tell Deziree."

Did I relish the thought of telling Dezi multiple pieces of big ass news? Not at all. If for no other reason than it would be a lot to take in, even if there wasn't a pregnancy involved. And I was grown enough to know that if she got upset, it wouldn't be about me dating. Couldn't be, considering we all knew how happy she was about Izaiah.

But that was the point: we were all grown. Too grown for me to let the possibility of the reveal being slightly uncomfortable keep me from being with someone who made me happy.

Someone I could make extremely happy if she just gave me the chance.

And that was exactly how I explained it to Trina. I stayed silent after, letting my words sink in and settle over her. She was quiet for a while. A lot longer than I expected her to be. My pulse was thrumming with nerves and it felt as if my stomach was doing back flips.

When she finally spoke, she caught me off guard again. "You just have the answers to everything, don't you?"

"Not everything," I said cautiously. "Which is fine because I don't always have to have them." Gripping her chin, I added, "We're in this together. You know what that means, right?"

"We'll figure it out together," she said before tooting up her lips for a kiss.

I gave her what she was looking for after answering, "Exactly."

Trina

ONE OF MATTHEW'S best qualities was his ability to make everything sound so goddamn easy. His ability to make me *believe* that even though our situation might not be simple, it was manageable. It was a skill honestly, considering the fact I'd been practically shitting myself for months over the prospect of Dezireé finding out what happened between us. And now with this additional complication, burying myself in the snow and just staying there had looked like a pretty good option. But now Matt had me thinking that maybe I was overreacting.

We're grown. We like each other. We'll figure it out together.

He gave me the same three reassurances repeatedly as we put the finishing touches on our little snow family. Lucky for him, he didn't need any artistic ability to do his day job because his snowman was piss-poor. The warm glow of safety he brought to my spirit, though... It was more than enough for me to let that go. After a little light teasing, of course.

"Got my hands out here numb as hell and you don't even appreciate the depth of my creativity."

The snort I let out at his words had him pouting even more. "Aww, don't be such a baby, baby." I didn't attempt to hide my giggle as he helped me out of my coat and hung it on the hook in the mudroom right next to his.

"Who's being a baby? I'm just saying you should appreciate me a little more, considering I was willing to catch frostbite for you." He held up his hands in demonstration.

I rolled my eyes at how unserious this man was being as if he hadn't just slipped off the thickest gloves I'd ever seen. Instead of calling him out on it, though, I simply took his hands in mine, rubbing them back and forth.

"Here, let me help."

Feeling bold as hell with no one else around, I guided his hands to my sweater, slipping them underneath the fabric until his cold palms were pressed against the warm skin of my back. The gesture brought us closer together as I slipped my own hands under his turtleneck.

"Does that feel better?" I asked, my voice taking on a husky quality. The prickling feeling across my skin had nothing to do with the chill of his fingers and everything to do with who they belonged to.

"It's a start," he said, his voice a whisper as he leaned in, forehead pressed against mine. It was so reminiscent of our moment yesterday that it was no surprise when my pulse began to race. Or had that thumping come from my pussy? It was so hard to tell when the scent and feel of him sent my thoughts racing.

"Correct me if I'm wrong, but—" His words stopped, cut off as he spun me around to lean me against the door. "But I think that mistletoe above us means one of us is owed a kiss."

"Is that a fact?" All it took was one quick glance to see that he was right. Not a surprise considering the array of holiday decorations that covered the cabin, but it was interesting that I hadn't even noticed it until Matt pointed it out. I couldn't help but wonder how many other doorways I'd overlooked with the small pieces of greenery. "Well, what are you waiting for, then?"

Funny how after going so long without experiencing the taste of Matthew's lips, within a matter of twenty-four hours it was like I couldn't get enough. Then again, I'd spent weeks—no, months—dreaming of those lips every time I closed my eyes.

I could feel his hard length pressing against my stomach as his hands tightened at my hips. The ache left over from last night's activities served as a reminder of just what that part of him was capable of.

"Matty." His name was a whimper on my lips as he gave me a brief reprieve to let out a groan of his own.

Before we had a chance to get lost in the kiss, the sound of a crash followed by a small shriek brought us back to the present.

"What the fuck?" I wondered aloud, still a bit dazed by the kiss.

"That sounded like Kamille." While I was still stuck in our mistletoe moment, his tone took on a worried quality.

"Christ, I swear her ass could get hurt even if she was wrapped up in a bubble."

Matthew snickered, knowing it was true. The girl had been accident-prone since birth. "You should probably go check on her. I'll heat up some of that leftover chili and cornbread."

Settling on a divide-and-conquer approach, we went our separate ways, me silently cursing Kamille for interrupting the moment.

"Girl, what are you—" Finishing that sentence wasn't even an option once I saw the scene laid out before me.

Or should I say once I saw Grayson laid out in front of me, with Kamille riding him like she was going for the grand prize.

"Oh my god!"

"Shiiiit!"

"Shut up!"

Three different exclamations from three different people for three very different reasons.

Exactly how much soap would I have to use to get the vision of my bestie coming on that man's dick out of my head? At least that's what it looked like was happening. It was a little hard to tell since she was covering his muffled cries with her hand. It also looked like when they hit the floor, they took the lamp on the nightstand with them.

What the fuck?

I hurried and shut the door, scurrying back to the kitchen as if distance was going to remove the image from my brain.

"Everything okay?" Matthew asked when I made it back to the kitchen. I must've looked completely unnerved because he came rushing around the island, a worried expression all over his face.

I scoffed, face turned up in disgust. "How about no. I just saw a lot more of my bestie than I've ever wanted to see in my life."

When his worry turned to confusion, I moved around him and leaned back against the counter. "Turns out that tension we've all been feeling for the last year from Kamille and Gray? Yeah, it was sexual tension. And they've decided to work it out in a very physical way."

There was about a sixty-second delay between the end of my

sentence and the dawn of understanding that fell over Matt, but once it hit him, he burst out laughing.

"Why is this funny to you?"

"For two reasons, mama." He closed the gap between us, easily lifting me onto the counter so that he could fit himself between my thighs. "One, from the way it sounded, Kamille might have literally fallen onto that nigga's dick, which is hilarious."

"Yeah, only because you're not the one who had to see it." I turned my lips down in a pout.

"Which brings me to reason number two, which is more of a question, I guess. You and Kamille roomed together for all four years at Oakwood U and you never once walked in on her handling her business?"

"Uhh, no!" It was clear he didn't believe me from the look he was giving me. "I'm serious! We had a whole system worked out. One we put in place because *she* walked in on *me* and we both agreed we never needed that shit to happen again."

Matt shook his head before placing a kiss on my neck. "So she just evened up the score."

"Please. That was years ago." It was on my mind to explain my reasoning further, but the sensation of his tongue gliding across my skin thoroughly distracted me.

What had I been saying?

"Okay, so maybe it's you who needs to even the score."

The way this man managed to coax me into lifting my hips so he could slip his fingers past the band of my cargos was so smooth, I hadn't even realized he'd done it until he made contact with my clit.

A hiss slipped through my lips as my hips gave an involuntary jerk and I felt him smile against my skin.

"Any objections to that plan?"

Why did he insist on sucking on my pulse point like that after asking me a question? And the nerve to do it at the exact same time he was framing my clit between two fingers, driving me up the wall—or counter, rather—with their attention to detail...

"Not at a-all, counsel—*ooooh shit*."

The fact that we were out in the open in the kitchen didn't register. The thought that Kamille or Grayson could easily walk in and see Matthew playing with my pussy didn't either. My mind and body had one single focus as Matt's lips connected to mine, his grip on the back of my head anchoring me in our hungry kiss.

One little orgasm wouldn't hurt.

Each of his ministrations had me convinced as I lifted my hips to meet his fingers.

A little too convinced.

"Surprise, bit—*ahhhhh!*"

The sound of that shriek snapped me from the stupor, though it apparently didn't prompt Matty to remove his fingers from their current home.

"Is that—"

"Dezi," I said, finishing his sentence.

Shit.

| FRIDAY |

"DASHING THROUGH THE SNOW, with a hoe ass nigga named Gray. Over the cliff he'll go, if he doesn't stay out my way!"

Somebody get the Grammy ready because I was absolutely killing the rendition of the opening lines of "Jingle Bells" I'd created on the ride up to the cabin. Actually, make that two Grammys: one for vocal ability and the other for songwriting. Now all I needed was a bit of choreography and we'd have a triple threat on our hands.

"Cute. Real cute," said the voice behind my creative inspiration. It was about time he inspired something other than my gag reflex.

Wait… That didn't come out right.

"Cuter than you, that's for damn sure," I said, not bothering to hide the irritation in my voice. Grayson could breathe wrong and it would get on my damn nerves. Shit, the fact that he was breathing at all was an inconvenience. And it pissed me off even more that it was so damn easy for him to get under my skin.

Was I known to pop off on people now and then? Oh, for sure. I was affectionately known as the friend people called when they needed someone cussed out.

But no one—and I mean *no one*—ever seemed to set me off like Grayson.

Don't act like you don't know why that is.

Ignoring the very unnecessary voice in my head, I looked up to see something even more annoying: Grayson smiling.

It widened as he gave the chili a stir, watching me the entire time. "You're a lot of things, beautiful, but a liar has never been one of them."

Instead of replying, I narrowed my eyes in irritation. Why had the universe cursed me with a best friend whose brother also happened to be the spawn of hell?

A demon who was also fine as hell, as much as it pained me to admit. Too fine for his own good.

It wasn't even that he was my type. I didn't have a type, honestly. I loved men of all shapes, sizes, and complexions, and I knew as well as anyone that attractiveness was subjective. As unbelievable as it may seem, every person I met did not, in fact, recognize how cute I was. Not everyone agreed with me that little booties mattered or liked my big, naturally curly hair, damn near flawless cinnamon brown skin, or slim frame.

Which obviously meant they were lacking in taste, but that wasn't the point.

The point was that objectively, Grayson was fine as fuck. He was *everybody's* type.

Wavy locs that stopped past his shoulders, deep bronze skin, perfect white teeth framed by a neat goatee, and a chest that had to be chiseled out of marble and covered in tattoos. All this packaged up in a nigga that stood six foot two and looked like he could bench over two-fifty. Scratch that, he could absolutely bench over two-fifty.

Did I mention the gold hoop in his nose?

And the worst part about it was that he just knew he was God's gift to women.

The man's entire existence should've been deemed a crime.

Then again, maybe his cocky attitude was a saving grace. A blessing in disguise since it was the only reason I wouldn't let his ass touch me with a ten-foot pole. His or otherwise.

Oh, really? You sure about that?

"Is the chili done or not? You in here acting like a five-star Michelin chef over a basic ass firehouse recipe and meanwhile, I'm starving."

Letting the dig about his cooking go, Grayson focused on my original question. "Yeah, it's done. Matty didn't let y'all know when he went back to your room?"

"No, he was a little…preoccupied."

Right on schedule, a door slammed somewhere in the house—*mine, if I had to guess*—followed by what sounded like stomping up a set of stairs. So yeah, preoccupied was definitely the word.

"You wanna tell me what that's all about or should I start guessing?"

"You could start by minding your business," I snapped.

The details of what was going on between Trina and Matty wouldn't stay secret for long, especially if they decided to play happy home with their real-life Baby Alive, but that didn't mean

I was going to broadcast their business before they were ready. Especially not to Gray's ass. I wasn't quite sure how he would take the news that his little sister's ex had apparently been fucking on one of her best friends.

I'd like to at least give them a chance to figure it out before getting anyone else involved.

Probably a good thing Dezi and Izaiah are stuck somewhere else. For now at least.

"Just saying I'd like to know what I'm dealing with since we're all up here together. Especially if y'all decide to start plotting against me since I'm outnumbered."

His tone was teasing, but I refused to give him even the smallest smile. Even if his had my pussy on overdrive.

"And I'd like for you to choke, but we can't always get what we want, now can we?"

"Beautiful, I'd give you just about anything you want. All you have to do is ask."

Liar.

But I wouldn't say it aloud. No, saying it aloud would lead to a whole other conversation that I refused to have.

Never a-fucking-gain.

"How about you worry a little less about what everybody else in this house has going on and focus on not burning dinner? Bad enough you're cooking in the first place."

Grayson just chuckled as he turned off the heat and moved the pot to a different burner.

"Is this the part of the conversation where we act like niggas don't beg me to make my famous chili and cornbread combo around the firehouse?"

"No, this is the part where I point out that niggas in a firehouse have questionable taste in the first place, so their taste buds can't be trusted." A buzzing sounded from the double oven, a sign I assumed meant the cornbread was ready. Perfect.

Blowing by him, I grabbed an oven mitt and moved to pull it from the oven. As I set it on the cooling rack, I felt his body press in behind me.

"And now is the section of the program where you act like you didn't have multiple bowls of this shit the last time I made it for you."

"I'll eat anything when I'm hungry."

Which was only partially true. The full truth was his shit was some of the best chili I'd ever had, but he didn't need me to tell him that. His ego was big enough as it was.

"Didn't you ask me to bring you a special batch for your birthday last year?"

And see, now he was trying to be slick.

Yes, I had requested my own bowl, and he'd teased me about it then, but brought it anyway with a side of his usual flirtatious banter.

Only, the chili wasn't all I'd wanted that night. I'd asked for another gift for my birthday. One I whispered in his ear after pulling him into my bedroom and climbing into his lap. Oakwood might be a city, but the community was small. I'd heard more than a few times that the dick was bomb. And after years of pushing the boundaries and sending flirty jabs at each other, I was finally ready to see if all the talk was true.

It never crossed my mind that he'd tell me no. And not just a no, but a full-blown dismissal when he lifted me off his lap, shook his head, and left the room.

"Thanks, but I'm good on that, Kami," he'd said as he headed toward the door.

"You're good? What the fuck is that supposed to mean?"

"It means exactly what I said. I'm not interested in what you're offering. Happy birthday, though."

That was it. That was the last thing he said before disappearing, leaving me horny, tipsy, and fucking confused.

I was pissed off and embarrassed and tried my best to shake it off. But when I'd finally gone back to the party and saw him smiling in some other bitch's face, arm wrapped around her pulling her close, I lost my shit. Next thing I knew, rum punch was dripping from every inch of him and the bowl was dropping to the floor as I went to swing.

For him to have the nerve to allude to that night here and now? After playing in my face, flirting and fucking with me ever since? He had the wrong one.

"Grayson, if you don't get the fuck away from me, I swear I will burn your ass."

A few seconds passed—far too many for my liking— before he backed away.

"Whatever you say, beautiful."

We spent the next few minutes moving in silence, grabbing whatever we needed for dinner before fixing our respective bowls and heading into the living room with the TV. I had no clue what Matt and Trina were getting into upstairs, but I had a feeling they'd be a minute. And while there was no way in hell I was going to sit at a table and share a meal with this asshole, starving myself wasn't an option either.

So instead, I settled into one of the very comfortable chairs, food and the spiked cider I'd made earlier in hand, and pressed play on *Christmas with the Kranks*, one of my favorite holiday movies.

All while trying my hardest to act as if I couldn't feel Grayson's stare, smirk, or presence in the goddamn room with me.

Truth be told, he'd done me a favor that night. What the hell had I been thinking? Fucking around with Grayson was a bad idea, one induced by tequila and a birthday high.

I was not falling into that trap again.

grayson

THIS WOMAN WANTED to beat my ass.

If looks could kill, I would've been dead and buried multiple times over the last several hours. Kamille seriously did not fuck with me, and instead of pissing me off or setting the tone for me to stay away from her, all it did was make my dick hard as a motherfucking brick.

What did it say about me that the threats were what turned me on?

That you're one sick ass nigga for real.

Maybe so, but there was something about the slim five-eight woman that made me want to test her limits and keep her attention on me at all times. It was part of the reason I made a point of fucking with her so much.

Did she get on my nerves? Hell yeah.

But aggravation only made up a third of the emotions I felt whenever she was around. The rest was pure attraction. Both Kamille's beauty and personality appealed to me on every level. And the truth was, as soon as she started hurling threats my way, the only thing I wanted to do was wrap my hand around her neck, throw her up against the wall, and fuck her five ways from Sunday.

Only when I had the chance last year, I'd fucked it up. Royally. Spectacularly. There probably wasn't a bigger fuck-up in the history of fuck-ups.

It hadn't even been intentional.

Nigga...

Yeah, that was a lie. I meant that shit and then immediately wanted to kick my own ass after I did it. My ego wouldn't let me, though. Not after spending half the night watching her giggle and hang all over Jeremy, a nigga from the firehouse that was only there because I'd invited him. Second biggest regret of the night.

Kamille wasn't mine in any way, shape, or form, but seeing a nigga who barely carried his weight around the fucking station touch her, flirt with her, acting like it was his mission for the night to lay up with her fucked me up. It made zero sense considering he wasn't the first or the last nigga I'd ever seen flirt with her. I'd known Kamille her entire life, watched a gang of niggas practically line up for the chance with her since high school. Sometimes it didn't bother me and I didn't think twice about it. Then there were times like that night, where seeing the shit made me want to punch a hole in the goddamn wall.

So when she led me to her bedroom and came on to me in a way I'd been dreaming about for as long as adult Grayson could remember, instead of giving her the birthday gift she was craving, I put my goddamn foot in my mouth and told her thanks, but no thanks.

What do you want from me? The streets said I was fine, not smart.

And then instead of coming to my senses and going right back into the room, I had to make shit worse and flirt with some random just to prove to myself I could.

I never saw the bowl of rum punch coming, but I should have.

And if I thought there'd been any chance of apologizing and getting another shot in the days that followed, it must've been delusion feeding that dream because what had once been flirty, snarky banter turned into full-on hate.

But there was a thin line between love and hate, right? Or was it hate and lust?

Either way, the more Kamille tried to prove she despised me, the more I was sure it was the complete opposite. She was trying too hard to convince me otherwise.

Like I said, twisted and delusional. But a nigga had to have dreams, right?

Matt and Trina volunteered to clean the kitchen after dinner. I was already on my second bowl of chili when they finally made it downstairs, both sneaking glances at one another as if we wouldn't notice. It didn't take a rocket scientist to guess what they'd been up to. Not that I cared since they were both grown as fuck, but they needed to get a handle on that shit before my sister showed up. Dezi was cool and my best friend may have been making her happier than I'd seen her in a really long time, but that didn't mean she wouldn't get here and cuss everybody out if she saw something she didn't like.

After heading up to my room to shower and throwing on a pair of sweatpants and a t-shirt, I grabbed my phone and a blanket and headed back downstairs. As nice as the house was, the only room with a TV was the living room. Guess they were really leaning into the mountain getaway vibes of it all. And that was cool, people needed to unplug and shit, but while everyone else was turning in early, I wasn't quite ready for the night to be over. Catching the highlights from the Challengers game would keep me occupied for a while.

As I made my way downstairs and into the living room, ready to set myself up on the couch, it became clear real quick I wasn't the only one who wasn't ready to head to bed. There Kami was, dancing around the kitchen as she sipped what I guessed was spiked apple cider as she slid an oven mitt over her hand.

"I thought I was imagining the smell of gingerbread." I tossed the blanket on the couch and made my way over in her direction.

Kamille had been working on the dough for her signature cookies since we'd gotten here and settled in. When I offered her space to make them while I worked on the chili, she just ignored me and went about her business, so I'd assumed she wasn't making them until tomorrow. Turns out she'd just been waiting for me to get the fuck out of her way.

Surprise, surprise.

She'd changed into a little long-sleeved and shorts pajama set covered in—you guessed it—gingerbread men. It was no surprise that without a stitch of makeup, hair up in a messy bun, and glasses on her face to replace the contacts she always wore, she was still one of the baddest women I'd ever seen in my life. Here I'd been thinking Trina had Matt following her around like a little puppy and I was ready to do the exact same for the woman in front of me. As she turned around to open one of the oven doors, I couldn't help but suck in a breath.

Shit. The way her little ass cheeks were peeking out from under the shorts had me readjusting myself in my pants. Lil' baby did not play fair.

"Damn, Kami. We might have to find you a job in Santa's work-shop with the way you in here getting shit done." In the time I'd been handling my business upstairs and bullshitting, she'd already made what looked like four batches of cookies. She was working on the next one as I came around the counter and stole one off the cooling rack.

"Uh-uh!" She took a swipe at me, but it was too late. He'd already lost his head. "Who told you that you could have one of my cookies?"

I smirked as her words took on a different meaning than the one I knew she intended. "You didn't say I couldn't. But if you're trying to offer up a different set of cookies, I'll gladly make the trade."

Her eyes narrowed in the same way they always did when she wanted to smack the shit out of me. My dick got even harder.

"You're disgusting."

"I've been called worse." A better man might have taken the hint and left her alone. Good thing I never claimed to be a good man, let alone a better one. "You might find out you actually like it if you gave it a try for yourself."

She scoffed, rolling her eyes and turning to put what looked like the last two trays of cookies into the oven. "In your dreams, Grayson. You couldn't pay me to touch you, let alone kiss you."

"I seem to remember you saying something very different not too long ago."

See? My dials were automatically set to asshole. It was like I couldn't turn it off.

This time when she turned around, the heat in her gaze really could have set me on fire. In a split second, she smacked me clear across the fucking face. The burn was instant. I hadn't expected the force behind it to snap my head the way it did, but damn, her ass was stronger than I thought.

"Aye, Kamille, I let you get away with a lot of shit," I said, heaving out a sigh, jaw clenched. "But I'm not one of those niggas that's about to let you put your hands on me just 'cause you think you can."

"Let me? Grayson, you don't let me do a damn thing. I'm a grown ass woman, so you can kiss my ass with all that bullshit you talking. If you want me to keep my hands to myself, then keep your comments to yours."

All the fucking talking she was doing was going in one ear and out the other. I could see her mouth moving, but the problem was all I could seem to focus on were her lips, not the words.

Plump and heart-shaped, I just knew they had to be soft. If I kissed her right now, what would they taste like? Would the flavor of the cider be in the forefront or would the whiskey I knew was mixed in slip through and be the star of the show? Did she like her bottom lip nibbled on? Shit, would she bite or suck on a nigga in the middle of a kiss?

Every single one of those questions flowed through my head as she proceeded to list all the things wrong with me. At least I thought that's what she was doing. Like I said, the words were barely registering.

Only one way to find out.

It took two strides to close the distance between us. Ten seconds for my hand to grip the back of her neck as I pulled her in and pressed my lips to hers. And a full thirty for her to kiss me back after standing there frozen because she'd been caught so off guard. But see, that's how you had to do shit with Kamille. If you let her think for too long, she'd go down a rabbit hole that she may never come out of. Fuck all that. Let's be present in the moment and see what this shit was really hitting on.

At least that's what I told myself to rationalize and justify my actions.

And anyway, it turned out I was wrong. She didn't taste like cider or whiskey. I mean the traces were there, but as I sucked on her tongue, earning myself a moan in the process, the biggest flavor hitting me was gingerbread.

Should've known she'd been in here dipping into her own stash.

Just as I was hitting my stride, hand reaching down to cup her ass, it was like the movement broke the spell because the next thing I knew, she was shoving me away. Unlike the smack she'd delivered earlier, this didn't have as much force as she intended, but I stepped away anyway. No need to push my luck any more than I already had. But goddamn was it tempting.

"Don't you ever do that shit again."

Kamille's voice was a hiss, letting me know she was dead serious. Or at least she wanted to be. This time when I looked into her eyes, it wasn't an angry glare she was sending my way. No, this heat was different, and it called out to me just like it had that night on her birthday.

"You got it, beautiful. Don't worry."

I grabbed another cookie, holding it up in thanks, and backed away toward the living room.

"Next time I put my lips on you, it'll be because you asked for it. And trust me, lil' baby. You'll definitely be asking for it."

Camille

THAT COCKY MOTHERFUCKER.

This nigga had lost his mind. Who the fuck did he think he was, kissing me like that? Sucking on my tongue like I was the most delicious thing he'd ever tasted. Squeezing my ass, which apparently fit perfectly in the palm of his hand, like he was staking his claim. Making my pussy so wet I was sure there had to be a wet spot on my shorts telling all my damn business.

The fucking audacity.

Fuck him.

I mean, you could. Just for research.

No. Fuck no. Hell no. Not an option.

Not even a teeny one?

I shoved the one-person argument from my mind as I grumbled, cussing Grayson out under my breath, wishing I could slam my door a second time for dramatic effect.

Fucking Grayson wasn't an option because I wasn't some weak-in-the-knees ass bitch who folded and dropped her draws just because some fine ass nigga knew what to do with his mouth.

And anyway, it couldn't be a "teeny" anything because wasn't a damn thing small about what I'd felt in his pants.

How the fuck did that man lug around all that goddamn life-saving equipment when he was also carrying a third leg?

The daze I'd fallen into after feeling it proved he was a walking fire hazard. Why else would I have almost burned that last batch of cookies?

God. Leave it to Grayson to go and ruin a perfectly good ginger-bread cookie baking session.

I'd perfected the recipe with my aunt years ago in high school. As soon as a chill appeared in the air, gingerbread people started appearing out of nowhere, overpopulating my kitchen, work, Dezi's law firm. Shit, Trina got care packages at least twice a month, and I made sure to drop some off at the firehouse too. Just not for Grayson's benefit. At least not after last year.

And yet his ass still ended up with a taste, didn't he?

I groaned, pissed with myself all over again. All I'd wanted to do was bake some damn cookies, drink my cider, and curl up in bed with my iPad to watch another movie.

Instead, I was lying here, aggravated and horny, while I could still hear *SportsCenter* playing faintly from the living room.

Was he going to be out there all night? Fuck, I hoped not. If the universe was kind, he'd take his ass back upstairs and let me fuck myself in peace.

Because I was absolutely about to fuck myself to sleep.

I knew bringing my favorite vibrator on this trip was a good idea. Plugging it in to charge when we'd first arrived was an even better one. Resigning myself to tuning out every other noise, I lowered the lights, leaving only the dim glow of the lamp casting shadows along the wall, and closed my eyes as I burrowed deeper under the covers, letting the warmth of the room relax me.

It started slow.

My fingers traced along the inside of my bare thigh, skimming along the edge of my shorts. The other hand reached up, cupping one breast under the matching shirt, the coolness from my skin causing me to hiss on contact. I wished like hell another picture would form in my mind, but there was only one face I could see as I rolled one hardened nipple between my fingers, as the other hand dipped below my shorts.

Grayson.

He was leaning over me, nose ring glinting in what little light there was as his lips pressed against the inside of my throat.

"Is that pussy wet for me, lil' baby?"

I gave a quick nod as one finger split my lips, finding my pussy hot, slick, and sticky even though things were just getting started.

Fuck, what would it feel like to have his fingers, strong and thick, circling my clit right now?

Applying just a little more pressure, the Grayson my imagination conjured up placed one hand over mine, whispering the complete opposite of sweet nothings in my ear.

"This pussy would look so good taking my dick, beautiful. I could stretch you out so perfectly if you let me."

Biting my lip to muffle the sound of my moans, I continued to stroke my clit, sending shots of electricity up my spine.

"I bet you taste so fucking good. Maybe I should get on my knees and find out."

This time it was a whimper that escaped as I twisted under the covers, pleasure flooding every one of my senses. The vision of Grayson doing exactly that, getting down on his knees, ready to worship me had me pulling my fingers from my pussy and reaching for the dark blue dildo next to me. I wasted no time turning it on, the vibrations triggering a sigh of relief. The moment the tip touched my clit, I sucked in a breath, back bowing off the bed.

"Shit!" I gasped aloud, no care or concern about the possibility of someone hearing me. I was in my own world. One where one of the finest, most aggravating men I'd ever met was looking up at me through those long lashes of his, encouraging me to get my nut any way I could.

"Does it feel good, beautiful?"

"Yes." The word was a whisper on my lips, but he apparently wanted more.

I was aching, thighs slick, pussy empty and fluttering. God, it felt good, but something was missing. I needed more.

"Let me see how well you can take it."

Eagerly placing the toy at my entrance, my hips shifted as I slowly worked in the smooth shaft, taking inch after inch. And when it started to vibrate against my walls...

My god, it felt so fucking good.

"Grayson," I whimpered, his name a song on my lips.

"That's right, Kami. Tell me how good it feels to fuck that pretty pussy of yours."

Tell him? Why would I need to say anything when I knew he could hear it for himself? Each flick of my wrist, each thrust of the silicone dick brought a new wave of pleasure. Another round of sobs I was trying my hardest to muffle in the pillow as I fucked myself with no concept of anything else except what was happening between my thighs at the very moment. And the vision of the man who was making it happen.

The last words he'd said to me before leaving the kitchen flashed across my mind.

"And trust me, lil' baby. You'll definitely be asking for it."

God, I hated how right he was. I could picture that cocky grin of his clear as day, daring me to ask for what I wanted.

So I did.

"Grayson, please." I was whining now, desperate for release. "Please make me come."

The voice that answered came loud and clear. Too real for it to have been conjured by my imagination.

"I thought you'd never ask, beautiful."

grayson

WAS THAT...

Reaching for the remote, I hit mute, creating a cone of silence in the room. I could've sworn I'd heard something but couldn't quite put my finger on what it was or where it'd come from. When I didn't hear it again I shrugged, chalking it up to the wind.

"I've heard of wind moaning before, but not like that," I muttered to myself, settling back against the couch pillow to focus on the highlights playing on the screen.

When the same sound started up again just a few minutes later, I knew I wasn't tripping. Those *were* moans I was hearing; the only question was where were they coming from. Were Matt and Trina going at it again already or…

No, those sounds weren't coming from upstairs. They seemed a lot closer, and since they obviously weren't coming from me after I'd decided only a nigga without any home training would fuck his hand on the couch where anyone could see, that left one other option.

Oh shit. Kamille.

As my brain put two and two together, my body went into autopilot, propelling me off the couch and down the hallway leading to her room. I stopped just shy of the door, practically holding my breath.

"Ooooh shit."

My body instantly tensed at the sound as I braced my hands against the wood frame. Just a few feet away on the other side of the door was the woman of my literal dreams, and by the sound of it, she was on the verge of coming. Every muscle in my body was screaming at me to move. To do something as all the possibilities of what was happening in that room flashed before my eyes.

Was she using her fingers or had she brought a toy with her? I strained my ears but couldn't pick up on any buzzing, just more moans. Each one seemed to break down what little restraint I had second by second. What was she picturing as she played with that pretty pussy of hers? I may have never laid eyes on it, but I already knew it was perfect, just like the rest of her.

"Grayson."

Did she just…

It was my name on her lips as she fucked herself. Which meant it was my fingers, my mouth, my dick currently fueling her fantasy.

Fuck restraint. It was overrated.

There was only a small amount of hesitation in my movements as my hand gripped the doorknob, twisting it slowly as I pushed the door open. The room wasn't pitch black, thank god. A golden glow stretched over the room, intensified by the light from the hallway behind me.

Part of me thought my sudden entrance into the room would destroy the moment, jolting her out of the pleasure-induced fog she was currently in, but by the look and sound of things, it hadn't dawned on her that I was there.

With her eyes closed and her hand buried beneath the comforter, I could only imagine what she was doing, but I had the perfect view of the top half of her, shirt pushed up and breasts exposed as she played with her nipples.

My mouth had literally run dry and all the blood raced toward my dick as it hardened at the sight of her. She was so fucking gorgeous. And as she called my name again, I swear my heart stopped beating, just for a split second.

"Grayson, please."

She was whining now, eyes still closed and face half-buried in one of the pillows. She'd managed to kick the comforter down enough where the dark vibrating toy she was using was visible. I could just make out the creamy coating that covered it as she pumped it in and out of herself, legs beginning to shake, each thrust more forceful than the last.

"Please make me come."

All reason and common sense went out the window. I didn't think about the fact that I shouldn't be here right now. Didn't contemplate whether or not this was the smart thing to do. Once again, my feet seemed to have a mind of their own, sending me over to the side of the bed until I could see every inch of her clearly.

"I thought you'd never ask, beautiful."

Kamille's eyes flew open as she stared at me with a shocked expression on her face.

"Grayson! What the fu-fuck are y-y-yo—*oooh my god!*"

Though she'd started to sit up, probably to cuss me out, her head immediately fell back against the pillow as the vibrator sent her barreling toward the orgasm she'd just been begging for.

I couldn't take my eyes off of her. The image of her, hips winding, mouth open, eyes rolling into the back of her head as the rest of her face contorted with pleasure would be burned into my mind until the end of time. It'd take a miracle and a prayer to make me forget and I wasn't asking for either.

"Shit, lil' baby. You did that so fucking well, I think you deserve another one."

"Fuck. You." Both words sounded like their own individual sentence now that she seemed to be out of breath. "Who the hell told you to bring your ass in here?" she hissed.

I smirked, reaching out a finger and brushing it along her shoulder. "You did, gorgeous. Or did you forget how you were moaning my name while you played with yourself? Should I remind you?"

Kamille had never looked so flustered. It was like she wanted to cuss me out and hide all at the same time. From where I stood, there would be plenty of time for both later.

"Fuck you," she spat.

"Shit, I'm more than ready. Just say the word."

"Oh my god, get out!" Her hands flew up in protest as she sat up, bringing the dildo into view. My tongue snaked out, sliding across my lips as I looked at it hungrily. It was covered in her cum.

I leaned down, one hand pressed against the bed as I grabbed hers, bringing the toy to my lips. "How about you share first? Just a little taste."

With my eyes staring straight into hers, I wrapped my lips around it, the taste and smell of her both intoxicating as fuck. Not being the least bit worried about how I looked at the moment, I loosened my throat, letting her flavor settle on my tongue as I sucked greedily.

The way her mouth dropped open after she'd just managed to close it would've been comical if I wasn't so turned on. Did she realize she was fucking my throat right now? And I meant actively fucking it, since she'd started to move it in time with the bobs of my head.

"You never mentioned you were so greedy, Grayson."

Her pupils dilated as she thrust back and forth into my mouth. I groaned, reaching into my pants and giving my dick a hard squeeze as pleasure shot through me.

"You never asked," I huffed once I came up for air.

She shifted, pulling herself up on her knees and dropping the toy so her hands were empty when she grabbed either side of my face for an equally greedy kiss. It was almost like tasting herself on my tongue sent her into overdrive and made her forget she'd wanted to kill me just a few moments before. I snatched off her shirt, needing to feel her bare skin and cup her breasts in my hands.

"Is this a good time to tell you your tits are fucking perfect?" My thumbs brushed across both stiffened nipples and I felt the sudden urge to take them into my mouth and see if they tasted like caramel. So I did.

"Shut *up*." The last word was a hiss as I took my time suckling one and then the other, letting loose an appreciative groan that filled the room.

I wanted to protest when she yanked my head back up—didn't she know not to interrupt a nigga when he was worshiping a woman?—but shut up when she moved to push away my sweatpants and freed my dick.

The pleasure I felt at the sight of her leaning down was only outmatched by the pure need I felt when she placed a soft kiss on the tip. A nigga had died and gone to the fucking pearly gates. Where else would some shit like this happen?

And just as I'd done just a few moments before, she parted her lips, taking my dick down her warm throat as I swore.

"Shit, Kamille. That's...*goddamn*."

My hand flew to the back of her head, burying my fingers in her coils as I began to fuck her throat. Every thrust sent a tickle up my spine. She was looking right at me, the sound of her gagging filling the room as her eyes watered. But she was taking everything I was giving her.

"Fuck, you're beautiful," I groaned. And she was, with her back arched, ass pushed up in the air as she tried to suck the life out of me. And it was working. The moment I felt her hands cup my balls, I knew I was a goner. There was no surviving this. I hoped everyone in my life knew how much I loved them because Kamille Grady was sending me to an early grave.

Just as I was about to come, she pulled back, licking her lips and gasping for breath.

"Why would you...?" I nearly fell forward, weak in the knees as adrenaline pumped through my body.

Was she about to leave me here, dick hard, balls tight, forcing me to finish myself off? I'd gladly do it, especially if she watched.

"You don't come until I say so," Kami said, a glint in her eyes as she reached into the bag on her dresser, pulling out a condom. "And you owe me one more before you do that."

A grin spread across my face. "Pretty sure I can handle that."

I made quick work of rolling the condom on, ready to give her exactly what she'd asked for. Only when I looked up and saw her face down, ass up, a guttural sound slipped from my lips. One that was outmatched by the moan I let loose as I slid into her wet ass pussy.

What the fuck had I gotten myself into?

Camille

| SATURDAY |

TURNS OUT, *I really am a weak-in-the-knees ass bitch.*

Not even an hour after swearing up and down I wouldn't be caught dead fucking Grayson, I let him bend me over and fuck me six ways from Sunday.

What was I supposed to do after he'd let me fuck his throat with my favorite dildo just so he could taste me on it? Was I supposed to put his ass out after he fucked my throat in return? Yeah, that wasn't going to happen. I was too keyed up for any post-nut clarity to prevail.

Like I said, weak ass bitch.

But the dick was so damn good.

That was an understatement. Admittedly, the first round was over fast. As in a few strokes in and Grayson was coming so hard that I swear his grip on my hips had left a bruise. It was disappointing to say the least, but I told myself finding out Grayson was a quick pumper firsthand was the best way to get over...whatever this was.

That's the dick everyone has been raving about? Mmmm. They need to get out more.

At least that's what I thought.

"So...I GUESS YOU CAN LEAVE NOW." WE WERE LYING BESIDE each other, him trying to catch his breath and me both happy and pissed off with myself for bringing him so close to that nut by sucking his dick in the first place.

"Leave?" He sounded confused as he sat up, locs falling in his face as he looked down at me. "Leave as in 'nigga, get the fuck out 'cause I never wanted you here in the first place' or leave as in 'take your ass back out to the couch so I can go to sleep 'cause a round two ain't in me'?

I laughed. "Considering that was barely half a round, I have plenty of energy left in me. You, on the other hand..." My eyes traveled over him skeptically even as he reached for another condom and climbed on top of me, propping one leg up on his shoulder. "You look like you're a one and done sort of guy."

Grayson chuckled and notched himself at my entrance, allowing his thumb to circle my clit the same way I'd been doing earlier. My breath stuttered, but I refused to close my eyes. I knew the challenge in his gaze matched the one reflected in mine.

"Trust me, beautiful," he said in time with the first thrust. "Looks can be deceiving."

AND HE WAS RIGHT BECAUSE I SWEAR HIS LETHAL DICK ASS HAD me climbing the fucking walls for god knows how long.

Minutes? Hours? Days? Weeks?

I'd completely lost all sense of time.

It came back eventually, but by then it was four in the morning and my entire body was drained. I was faintly aware of Grayson moving to the bathroom and coming back to clean me up. I didn't even have the energy to make some slick remark the way I wanted. Just turned and drifted off to sleep, vaguely aware of his arms wrapped around my waist and the warmth I felt as his body pressed into mine.

Who knew Grayson was a cuddler?

I sure as hell didn't. But when I finally did wake up, just past noon, he still had me wrapped in his arms, face tucked into my hair as he slept peacefully.

No, no, no, no, no. What did I do? And why did I want to do it again?

I'd let my pussy lead me astray and now I was paying the price.

Girl, stop with the dramatics. It was damn good.

Yeah, too good, and there was the problem. This man had blatantly brushed me off and become a perpetual pain in my ass. Even now, I could feel the heat rising in my cheeks out of embarrassment. Why would I have sex with a man who clearly didn't want me? Why had he even climbed into this bed in the first place?

"All that overactive shit you have going on in your mind is fucking up my sleep, lil' baby. Relax."

The request was simple. It was also just enough for me to latch onto to get over my embarrassment and skip right to anger.

"Oh, my bad. I tend to go into crisis mode when I realize I'm fucking with a nigga that doesn't want me. It can be a lot to take in, you know. Sorry if that's inconvenient for you."

I yanked away from him and sat up, needing to put some space between us. Just looking at him—relaxed without a care in the world as he opened his eyes and stretched, one arm still tucked under his head and a sleepy satisfaction etched onto his face— made want to choke him.

"What are you talking about? When the fuck did I ever say I didn't want your pretty ass?"

"Weren't you the one who brought up my birthday yesterday? I know you didn't forget."

"Nah, I didn't forget. Which is how I know the words 'I don't want you' never came out my mouth."

I scoffed. His ass was un-fucking-believable. "If you're just going to sit up here and lie to my face, you can carry your ass back to your room. Or to the living room. Or outside. Actually, you can carry yourself straight to hell for all I care." He had me all the way fucked up. I threw off the covers, climbed out of bed, and headed toward the bathroom, over both the conversation and him.

"Bruh, you're doing a lot right now, Kamille. Why the fuck would I lie?"

"Why do most niggas lie? For a piece of pussy."

When Grayson didn't respond right away, I took that as my sign I was right.

Should've known.

Sitting just beneath the surface was an emotion I didn't want to name, didn't want to give life to, but I knew it was hurt. So instead, I held onto my anger, praying that he would be gone by the time I came out.

It became apparent really quickly that no one was listening when I'd barely stepped a foot outside the bathroom before Grayson was crowding my space, pressing me against the doorframe. He had one hand on my hip while the other wrapped itself around my throat and gave it a light squeeze.

I fought the moan building in my throat as hard as I could.

Find a goddamn backbone.

The words were meant to put some steel in my spine, but the fresh wave of slick between my thighs told a completely different story about how his presence was affecting me.

"I was balls-deep in that perfect pussy of yours all night. Lying to get back in it seems counterproductive to me."

As if he needed to remind me.

I was still sore, but not so much so that I didn't clench my thighs to try and get rid of my ache for more.

"You turned me down." This wasn't just about reminding him. It was a reminder for me too.

Apparently he didn't need one either. "I know."

I threw my hands up in frustration and gave him a slight shove. Just like last night, it barely moved him, only caused him to drop his hold on my neck. "Okay, so what the fuck are we doing here, then? 'Cause you just said that didn't happen and now you're admitting it did. Whatever game you're playing, please take it somewhere else because I don't have the capacity for this bullshit."

"There is no bullshit and stop putting fucking words in my mouth. If you want to sit anything in this motherfucker, make sure it's that pussy. Shit, or maybe that blue dick you have lying around here since it turned you on so much."

"Fuck you."

This time instead of grabbing my neck again, he tightened his grip on my waist and dipped his free hand below the shorts I'd managed to pull back on. Or maybe he'd helped me into them before I fell asleep. It was hard to remember.

Especially since one of his fingers was currently fucking into me.

"Shit," I gasped.

"Now that I have your attention…" The confidence in his tone only made me wetter. My pussy really was a traitor. "Let's get a few things straight right quick. I never, ever said I didn't want you. Not then and not now. What I said was I wasn't interested in what you were offering, and I wasn't. Not at that moment anyway."

"That's fu-fucking semantics," I managed to get out as my hand wrapped around his wrist. Not to try and get him to stop, but to make sure he kept going.

"Maybe so, but when I said it, I didn't actually mean that shit."

"S-So you just go around saying shit you d-don't mean?" At this rate I was going to chew through my lip trying to hold back my moans and whines, but it wasn't working.

"I do when I'm irritated as fuck about you smiling in some other nigga's face, acting like you were going to give him the pussy we both wanted to be mine. So I put my foot in my mouth and fucked up."

My eyes fluttered closed as his thumb slid across my clit, spreading my juices all over the sensitive spot.

"But since apparently what happened last night wasn't clear enough to rectify that situation and whatever misconceptions you have in your mind, let me make myself clear."

Moving his hand from my hip, he used it to tip my head up until I was looking directly at him.

"I want you, beautiful. So bad I can fucking taste it. I want you as often as you'll let me have you, in whatever capacity you want to give yourself to me." Grayson leaned in more, dragging his tongue across my bottom lip, not even attempting to hide his own moan. "And right now, I want your cum all over my fingers. So you might as well start there."

He bent his fingers just enough to hit the special spot that had my knees buckling as my nails dug into his skin.

It was like I'd just made the drop on a rollercoaster as my stomach did a backflip and my toes curled. I might have even hit the floor if Grayson hadn't made a point to wrap his arms around my waist even as he continued to thrust his fingers into me. My walls spasmed around them, every muscle in my body wound tight until I had no choice but to relax into him, cum trickling down my thighs and his hand.

"Looks like you can follow directions after all."

I huffed a laugh and tried to straighten. "Are you going to let me taste it?" I asked as he brought his fingers into view, "or do you want it all to yourself again?"

The way he parted my lips and told me to suck was answer enough.

We carried on the same way for the next few hours, neither of us able to help ourselves or show any restraint. Other than a brief interruption from Matthew—who I prayed hadn't heard all the noise Gray was making behind me— and a shower which in itself turned into me dropping to my knees and Grayson shooting his cum down my throat before he fucked me against the shower wall, we couldn't seem to keep our hands off each other.

No, that wasn't true. We'd fallen asleep after the round in the shower. The nap had done my body good.

Waking up to Grayson, face deep in my pussy, had done it even better. Which was how I found myself bouncing on his dick for the second—no, third—time since we'd woken up that morning.

"Ohmygod, Grayson, stop fucking talking," I groaned as my hips rocked back and forth, causing the perfect amount of friction against my clit as they did.

"But you're riding this dick like it was made for you, beautiful. And you look so fucking good doing it too."

I was and I did, but shit, why did he have to say it out loud?

A nigga who could talk me through it did something to me every time, but the problem was I figured out I loved it when Grayson did it a little too much. My pussy tightened, so wet it was dripping, making a mess of both of us, and the more he talked, the worse it got.

I was sobbing and whimpering all over the place, hands planted firmly on his chest. *Goddamn,* the way he was fucking up into me felt so amazing I didn't even care that somehow, we'd ended up on the floor, lamp broken next to us.

"Ride that shit, lil' baby. *Fuck!*"

My body began to shake and the room began to spin. If we kept this up, I would never come up off this man's dick, and that was something dangerous. I should care, but all I could seem to focus on was the way his dick had begun to twitch as his eyes rolled to the back of his head and his hand reached up to pull at my nipples.

Somewhere in the distance, a door opened. A little nagging voice told me my voice wasn't the only one colliding with Grayson's as we came, but I couldn't bring myself to care. Everything just felt too fucking good.

I collapsed on top of him, completely out of breath. "I hate you." Him *and* the empty feeling between my thighs as we shifted and he slipped out of me.

He huffed out a laugh, trailing kisses along my neck as I tried—and failed—to lift myself off of him. "You keep telling yourself that, Kami. Your pussy is saying something different."

Groaning, I buried my face in his chest. "She's weak. You can't trust a thing she says."

"Yeah, well, I love the way she talks to me, so excuse me if I decide to stick with her."

Rolling my eyes, I sat up, moving just enough to climb up onto the bed as he followed. "Just so we're clear, all this dick you've been slinging doesn't make up for the shit you did last year."

"Oh, I'm well aware," he said, stretching and pushing his locs from his face. "But it's been fun trying."

Despite myself, I laughed, but before I could respond, a scream came from outside.

"What the fuck?" I muttered. Standing on my own wasn't easy, but I somehow managed, slipping on a pair of underwear and an oversized shirt. "Open the window and get some air flowing in here."

I took a look at him, dick out, body glistening with sweat.

Get a grip!

"And put some clothes on. I'll be back."

The smirk on his face was aggravating as hell, but I did my best to ignore it as I flew out of the room, rushing to see what all the noise was about. Only once I entered the kitchen, I was suddenly wishing I'd stayed right where the fuck I'd been.

"Tini, are you o— Dezi!"

The vibes in the room were all over the place, but the irritation rolling off of Dezireé was palpable.

What the fuck did I just walk into?

Snow & Tell

| FRIDAY |

HOW THE HELL do you ruin a trip before it's even really started?

Agree to work an overnight shift the day before what's supposed to be your first day of vacation. A vacation you've been planning with your girlfriend for months.

Oh, and make sure after you work that shift, you're late picking up said girlfriend so that by the time you get on the road, you find yourself stuck in traffic and inevitably get caught in a fucking snowstorm before you're halfway up the mountain.

A-plus job, Izaiah. Always going the extra mile.

No matter how many times Deziree repeated the phrase "I'm not upset," I didn't believe her. Or maybe I did and the problem was even if she wasn't upset, I was.

We could be wrapped up in front of the fireplace with a bowl of Grayson's chili right now.

That was the only thing running through my mind as we crept slowly along the road, windshield wipers on full speed and heat blasting.

"I'm gonna need you to fix your face, Zay."

"There's nothing wrong with my face, Zee."

I could feel her eyes on me, giving me the "nigga, please" look she'd perfected. "Try again. You've been pouting for the last thirty minutes for no reason."

Taking my attention off the road—because shit, it's not like we were moving much anyway—I looked over at the finest woman I'd ever seen who, unlike me, had a smile on her face like she found my attitude funny as hell.

"I'm—"

"And if you apologize one more time, I will haul off and swing on your ass."

That pulled a laugh out of me because I knew she was dead ass serious. My baby had hands. "Damn, woman, chill out. I ain't said it that much."

The look she gave me said otherwise.

"Okay, fine, maybe I have. My bad." Her hand shot out, popping me on my arm. "Ouch! I didn't even say the S-word! That was just because you're right, I've been going overboard saying it."

"Close enough."

"Yeah, whatever, Muhammad Ali. Just keep them hands to yourself. You know you hit hard as shit." I rubbed the aching spot to emphasize my point. "And I wasn't going to apologize again. I was going to say I'm annoyed as fuck. This wasn't how I wanted the weekend to go."

"Baby, I don't think anyone wants to be stuck in a snowstorm, but you've gotta stop acting like the entire trip is ruined. We're just delayed is all."

"You say that like there's a chance we're going to make it the rest of the way." The four-wheel drive on my truck had me tempted to give it a try, but the snow wasn't just coming down heavier, it was also starting to stick. If it was just me I had to worry about, I might've tried to keep going to see how far I'd make it, but trying that shit with baby girl in the car wasn't an option. No way was I about to play with her safety like that.

"Stop being so negative. I guarantee you if the snow stops within the next few hours, they'll be working overtime to get the roads cleared. By tomorrow night, we'll be right at the cabin with everyone else drinking spiked cider and playing naked Twister."

"Fuck makes you think I want to see your brother's naked ass in the air?" That was not a visual I needed floating around in my mind.

"It's a figure of speech." I didn't have to be looking at her to know she was rolling her eyes.

"Sure," I chuckled. Serious or not, Deziree had managed to ease my anxiety. A few minutes later, I took notice of a blue sign creeping up on the passenger side. "Looks like there's a lodge a few miles down the road. Can you—"

"Yep," she said, not needing me to say anything else.

Grabbing her phone, it only took a few minutes for her to call and see what they had available. While she did, I went ahead and changed the address in the GPS to what would hopefully be our new destination.

"Room at the AU Lodge secured," was all she said once she was done.

Cool. At least we wouldn't be stuck out here in the cold. "Thanks for taking care of that, baby girl."

"You really want to thank me?"

I recognized that tone of voice. Or rather my dick did, considering he bricked up quick as shit at the sound of it.

I turned my gaze in her direction and sure enough, she was giving me that look. The one that said *get on your knees and show me.*

"Pull over."

"Zee," I said, chuckling as I shook my head and focused my attention back to what was ahead of us. "It's fucking freezing and the roads are shit."

"What's your point?"

"That I can thank you just fine in a warm bed once we get to this lodge."

Instead of answering, I could hear her shuffling next to me. A quick glance and it was clear the noise I'd heard was her taking off her coat. Trying to split my attention between the road and her, I caught glimpses of what she was doing and goddamn, baby girl was serious. Had to be with the way she was slipping her sweater over her head, revealing a lacy bra that matched her amber brown skin perfectly.

Fuck.

"You in the habit of telling me no now, Zay?"

"Baby…" It was getting harder and harder to concentrate on driving. Realistically, we had about twenty, maybe thirty minutes left thanks to the weather. And while a nigga could wait that long, it was looking like my woman couldn't say the same. "It's not like I can just pull over on the side of the mountain, Zee."

Undoing her seat belt, she sat up until she was on her knees, leaning over to lick just along the side of my ear. "Pretty sure there's a rest stop coming up."

She was right. A sign appeared, almost as if the universe was conspiring with her to work against my good common sense.

And it was working.

Fuck it. Whatever this woman wanted, she was going to get, even if it sounded wild as fuck. Honestly, was your woman really your woman if you couldn't pull over and fuck her in the middle of a snowstorm like she asked you to?

izaiah

IT TOOK ALL of two minutes for me to pull off the road and into the rest area parking lot. By the looks of it, a few people were using it to regroup in this weather, but thankfully it wasn't hard to find a well-lit secluded spot where no one would be in our business.

While I was still trying to convince myself this wasn't the horrible idea I knew it was, Dezireé was sliding the passenger seat as far as it would go and climbing into the back of the truck. "You're really serious, huh?"

The smirk she wore on her beautiful face said yes.

And the way her finger traced along the cup of her bra silenced any and all critique I may have had. She was going to get whatever the fuck she wanted out of me.

Five months.

Five months was all it'd taken for me to become truly obsessed with this woman. If I thought she'd been the center of my attention before we'd hooked up at Kamille's party, the joke was on me. The shit was worse than ever now, but you'd never hear me complaining. It didn't matter how many times we found ourselves wrapped in each other's arms or how often I slid between her thighs, I could never get enough of her.

"You coming or what?" She tilted her head, a mischievous look on her face.

Not yet.

"Well, since you asked so nicely." Following her route wasn't an option. At six-two, doing anything back there was going to be difficult, but crawling back there was an absolute no. My truck had plenty of space, and she may have managed to climb her very thick, very fine ass back there with only a minor bit of difficulty, but I wasn't about to push my luck. I pushed open my door, slipped off my coat, and slid in beside her using a more conventional approach.

Between one second and the next, Dezireé's lips were colliding with mine.

Fuck, she tasted good. And the way her tongue swiped along my bottom lip just before tangling with my own? The groan that released deep from my throat told her everything she needed to know about what that shit did to me. Her arm wrapped around my neck as she leaned back against the window, pulling me down with her.

My own hands found their way to her waist and despite the heat blasting from the vents, she still gasped at their slight chill. The reflex allowed me to deepen the kiss, tasting the whimper that escaped as I deftly used one hand to undo her bra.

As much as I didn't want to, I pulled away, intending on taking my shirt off, but she stopped me with a shake of her head.

"Leave it on." I raised an eyebrow. "I like how rough it feels."

I still didn't understand until she pulled me back down, this time letting out a moan as the fabric from my sweater rubbed against her nipples.

Oh.

Bringing my lips down to hover over hers, I thought better of kissing her again, deciding instead to create a trail of kisses from her jaw to her neckline in that way I knew always had her pussy dripping for me.

The grip she had on me tightened, the possessiveness of it pulling at something in my chest and making my dick even harder. One hand found its way into her hair, pulling at her coils while the other undid the buttons on her jeans. Everything about her had me under a spell.

The taste of her tongue.

The feel of her skin as a shudder wracked her body when my hand dipped below her panties.

The sound of her gasp, desperate and throaty as my finger parted her lower lips.

It was all so fucking intoxicating that it was easy to forget about everything else happening around us.

Then there was the way she was looking at me, lids lowered with desire and bottom lip tucked between her teeth. A look like that would make any nigga feel like they were on top of the world, except I knew for a fact I was.

How could I not be when this was my woman? It didn't take a genius to know I was the luckiest nigga alive.

A lazy grin appeared on her face as she arched into me. "Are you just going to touch my pussy or do you plan to actually play with it?"

And there it was. One of her best qualities if you asked me: that mouth. Always ready to issue a challenge, no matter the situation.

"Your ass is fucking impatient, you know that?"

Rolling her eyes, Dezireé pushed me back enough that my hand slipped from its hiding place as she began to shimmy out of her jeans. "We're in the middle of nowhere in a snowstorm, Zay. Taking our time isn't a luxury we have."

My eyebrow ticked up as I reached out to help her out of the pants. "And whose fault is that?" My pants were the next to go.

"I plead the fifth," she giggled, wrapping one leg around my waist and taking my hand into hers. I didn't protest when she moved it right back to its previous position, this time sliding her panties to the side.

"Why am I not surprised?"

"Za—"

As much as I loved the way she said my name, it didn't compare to the moan she let out as I slid into her. She was slick and warm, her walls pulsing around the two fingers pumping in and out of her, almost like her pussy was welcoming me home.

I kissed both corners of her mouth before nipping at her bottom lip, using my thumb to play with her clit. Each swipe brought a new breath for me to swallow with a kiss. My lips moved down her throat, tongue snaking out to taste each sensitive spot along the way. I could hear her breathing grow ragged as I bit her neck, drawing a whimper from her. When she slid her hands under my sweater, I couldn't help but hiss at the feel of her nails scraping down my chest.

"I don't think I mentioned," I said, going back to trailing kisses along her skin, "just how good you look, Zee." Our gazes locked as my tongue dipped between her breasts.

"Maybe not today." Her breath caught in her throat.

"Shame on me, then."

I took one of her nipples into my mouth and immediately groaned at the way it stiffened after one simple lick. I'd never thought of myself as a breast man, but for Dezireé, I'd gladly take on the title. Hers were so heavy and perfect in my free hand that my grip tightened involuntarily. Moving to the other, I gave it the same treatment before blowing against it. The way she arched her back and let out a whimper had me puffing out my chest with pride.

"Well, I can promise you look as good as you fucking taste, baby girl." I drew my fingers out of her, just enough light filtering in from the outside to make out the sticky sweetness covering them.

Putting my multitasking skills into action, I lined my dick up with her entrance, giving it a stroke and spreading the precum across the tip. Her hips jolted as I tapped it against her clit.

I hung both cum-covered fingers above her lips. "Suck."

There was no question or smart ass remark at the command. Just Dezireé doing exactly as I said as my dick pushed into her and we filled the car with our moans.

Nothing about the position we were in was comfortable. I mean shit, we were grown as fuck. When was the last time I'd actually had sex in the back of a car? Had to have been years ago because it hadn't been in this fucking truck. There was no real reason to once I was old enough to have my own spot. Yet somehow this woman had me fighting for my life, ignoring the cramp forming in my calf and the slight pain in my lower back just so I could dig her out right here where anyone could see. The truck was rocking, windows were fogged up, and if anyone really cared to take a closer look, there was no doubt in my mind they'd know exactly what we were doing.

Fuck 'em. I didn't care.

I was too busy focusing on the bite of her nails in my skin and the wet heat between her thighs sucking me in deeper.

How did she always manage to get me into these compromising, public ass positions?

Why did I continue to let her?

Because you love her and she feels like fucking heaven.

The realization never ceased to amaze me. Two months had passed since we'd first said those three little words to each other and they still hit me in the chest so hard, my strokes faltered for a split second.

"I'm…shit…*shit*!" she called, snapping me from my thoughts as she flung one hand out, scrambling for purchase against the window. "Zay, please."

Her whines punctured the air, her body begging for release and hips rolling to meet each of my thrusts. And as this little escapade proved, whatever my baby girl wanted, she was going to get.

"Use your words, love."

"I need it." Her voice was thick with desire.

"And I'll always give you what you need. Isn't that right?" I wrapped one hand around her neck as the other held her hips in place, allowing me to fuck into her harder.

She nodded frantically, bottom lip wedged between her teeth as her head fell back, eyes closed tight as my pace quickened.

"You ready to come on this dick, Zee? Are you ready to make a mess for me?"

"Yeeees," she moaned and it sounded like perfection to my ears.

"Then give me that shit. Right now."

Whether it was the words, the dick, or a combination of the two I didn't know, but no sooner had I made my demand did she follow through like the good girl she was. She was practically choking my dick, walls tightening around me as her body shuddered, whatever words currently falling from her lips unintelligible.

Or maybe that was a result of the roaring in my ears as my balls tightened, her orgasm triggering my own as my cum coated her walls. "Fuck, fuck, fuck!"

Before my brain short-circuited, I sent a silent *thank you* up for her IUD because had it not been for that, I'm sure we'd have made a goddamn baby with this shit.

"Shit," I started once I'd caught my breath and my senses had come back to me, "think we have enough time to go again?"

deziree

WE, in fact, did not have time to go again. Not if we wanted to make it to the lodge before the roads were complete shit. I thought about it. Goddamn, did I think about it now that I knew Izaiah's backseat dick was more phenomenal than it had any right to be, but seeing how despite the extra snow that had fallen during our little commercial break, there was none falling at the moment, Izaiah and I both figured it was best if we saved round two for an actual room.

Not the worst idea in the world. And to be fair, having that fine ass man of mine on his knees in the shower while I gripped his locs and drenched his beard as he ate my pussy within an inch of his life—and mine—was absolutely worth the wait.

After being thoroughly fucked, washed, fed, and moisturized, the king-sized bed was calling my name.

"Considering how last-minute this was, this place is actually gorgeous," I said, admiring the cozy feel of the gold-accented room. I couldn't help but wonder which was more homey, here or the house we were supposed to be staying in with everyone else.

"Yeah, not a bad substitute for the night, honestly. Might be worth coming back later." With the heat on full blast in the room,

Izaiah was only wearing a pair of pajama pants as he slipped under the comforter. Then again, that may have been because I'd stolen the matching Oakwood Stallions t-shirt right out of his bag before he'd had the chance to grab it for himself.

I shifted, laying on my side so we were facing each other. It was so easy to get lost staring in those deep brown eyes of his. They were mesmerizing, just like the intricate tattoos that lined his forearms and the chocolate skin that would make any girl's pussy wet instantly.

Just one lick and we could start round three off with a bang.

"Depending on what this weather does, we might actually be stuck here the whole time."

His words snapped me out of my trance, even as my fingers reached out to trace along the wolf that covered his forearm.

"That might not be such a bad thing." My eyes flicked up to meet his. "You might actually get lucky again if it's just the two of us by ourselves," I teased. "Especially since staying here would mean not having to play referee between Kami and Gray."

A thought occurred to me. "But that also means there's no chance of you getting that security deposit back 'cause she'll probably put him through a wall if he plucks her nerves bad enough." Which we both knew he would. It was sick and twisted how much joy he got out of fucking with my best friend.

Izaiah groaned, wrapping his arm around my waist and pulling me in until our bodies were flush against each other. "How much time do you think we have before Kamille murders your brother?"

I let out a snort. "Let's just say if we're not there by tomorrow night, I'll have to get used to being an only child." My parents might not like the idea, but I could definitely make it work. After all, it'd been at the top of my Christmas list every year since I was five.

Clearly no longer concerned about the damage probably taking place at that very moment, Zay laughed right along with me. "Nah, we should have a little more time than that with Trina and Matt there. They should be able to keep them in their separate corners for another thirty-six hours."

"Assuming they aren't dealing with their own shit." Which they probably were if what I thought I knew was true.

As I snuggled in closer, loving how the warmth of his body seemed to melt mine, Izaiah's fingers followed a path only they seemed to know up and down my spine.

"Their own shit? Like what?"

I didn't say a word, choosing instead to bury my face in his chest as my lips formed a smile.

"Uh-uh, don't act like you can't hear me, Zee. I know your messy ass ain't about to tell me you set up this getaway knowing everyone on this trip had problems with each other except us. Ain't that nigga supposed to be one of y'all's closest friends or some shit?"

I leaned back just enough to look up and see the confusion written all over his face. "Now see, I ain't say shit about them having problems. Literally the opposite. Are you telling me you haven't noticed how weird Trina's been acting? Or how much time Matt has been spending up in New York for work?"

"Baby, I don't really spend my free time wondering what your old nigga is up to. As long as he's not smiling in your face anymore, I don't really give a fuck."

I rolled my eyes because we both knew if Matty was smiling in my face, it wasn't because he was trying to get this old shit back.

"No one is smiling in my face except you, baby."

"Yeah, you just make sure it stays that way. I'll knock a nigga's head off behind you. Remember that."

Remember it? The shit was committed to memory. Just the simple image the words conjured up in my brain made my pussy wet.

"So what are you saying? You think the two of them are fucking around?" He paused, narrowing his eyes in suspicion. "That's the reason you put this together? So you can either set them up or catch them doing some shit?"

I kissed my teeth. "Oh my gosh, shut up! Did you hear me say that?"

"Nah, but you ain't slick either. Your ass got a hidden agenda. It's written all over your face."

Smacking my lips, I crossed my arms, annoyed as hell. The nerve of my man to act like he knew me!

Girl...

Okay, so maybe I did do all this to get them in the same place. And maybe I was trying to push them together. So what? It wasn't like I really thought the two of them had done anything. In fact, I'd bet money that they spent most of their time being awkward as hell around each other. But it didn't take a mind reader to notice the way Trina's voice changed whenever Matty was brought up. Or the way he always seemed to have some cute, funny story to tell about the time they'd spent together whenever he was in town.

I wanted my girl to be happy, and even though it might be a little awkward and people may think it was weird and out of pocket, it wasn't far-fetched to think the two of them could be that for each other. Nobody else needed to understand my logic as long as I did.

"I'm only going to say this once, Zee. Mind your business and let grown folks do whatever they're gonna do."

"No clue what you're talking about." I turned around, pressing my back against his chest and sticking my ass out until my not-so-little friend was nestled up against it.

"Yeah, okay, play clueless if you want to. You gonna fuck around and either get your feelings hurt or start something you're not ready for playing in other people's shit."

"The only thing I'm ready for is bed," I said, adjusting myself in an attempt to get comfortable.

Something that sounded suspiciously like "lying ass" came from behind me as he accepted his role as the big spoon. I didn't pay him any mind, just let his presence relax me the way it always did as the day's events finally caught up to me. Whether Izaiah understood it or not, I knew exactly what I was doing. Now it was just a matter of wondering if I'd get to see my plan set in motion or if this weather would have me missing out on all the good shit.

deziree

| SATURDAY |

"SHOULD I say I told you so now or later? When would be convenient for you?"

Even though Izaiah was trying to act like he didn't feel me staring at him, the twitch in his cheek told me he was fighting back a smile.

"How about neither?" he snickered. "'Cause both would be annoying as hell, just like your little ass."

"First of all, ain't nothing little about me or my ass," I said, scrunching my nose in disgust even though it was clear he was joking. It was replaced by a smile. "And I may be irritating, but you still worship the ground I walk on."

A full burst of laughter filled the car. "Yeah, a'ight, you got me on that one."

We'd both slept in that morning, neither one of us in much of a rush to get out of bed, not to check the weather outside or the damage it had done. Instead, we took it upon ourselves to have breakfast in bed and engage in a little mid-morning head. Or rather I decided, since it was only right to return the very enthusiastic thank you Izaiah had given me the night before.

Once we did finally manage to pour ourselves out of bed, it became clear the snow had stopped overnight, giving the road crews plenty of time to clear a path up the mountain. At least that's what the front desk said when we called to see if we were good to check out or should try for another day.

Everything had gone exactly as I'd predicted.

Admittedly, now that we were on the road, I was feeling some type of way about not being able to run back the gingerbread waffles we'd eaten at breakfast and our decision to skip the walk around the property. We'd definitely have to come back at some point and make that happen. For now, though, I was happy we'd managed to have a safe trip over the last couple hours after getting the all-clear to get back on the road.

"Just admit you were worried for nothing yesterday and that I was right. In fact, we got the best of both worlds."

Careful of any slick spots that may have iced over, Izaiah made the final turn that would take us to our destination. "How do you figure?"

"We got to use the first part of the trip to spend some much needed quality time together, complete with a bomb ass breakfast and amazing sex without worrying about anyone hearing us. Now we get to spend the rest of it turning up with the crew and getting an early start on the holidays just like we wanted."

A mumbled response came from the driver's seat.

"What was that?" I teased, scrolling through my phone. The text I'd sent to the group chat with Trina and Kamille telling them we were on the way still hadn't gotten an answer. I'd managed to talk to Trina this morning to let her know we'd hopefully be headed up that way before it got dark, but we were going to make it a few hours sooner than I'd originally estimated.

"I said you're right, love. I don't know how I could have ever doubted your big, beautiful, know-it-all psychic brain."

I couldn't help but giggle at his teasing, letting him grab my free hand. A blush creeped up my neck as he kissed it and shot me a wink.

"Cute. Real cute."

Shaking my head, I pressed Kamille's contact picture. Straight to voicemail. Weird, considering it was usually glued to her hand at any given time of the day.

"Still no answer?"

"No. Shit, do you think reception is trash up there?" While Aurora Ridge wasn't necessarily in the middle of nowhere, between the storm and the altitude, it wouldn't shock me to find out service was spotty.

"It's possible, but you were able to get through this morning, right? And there weren't any problems yesterday."

"True. And it's not like we're far." If their service was knocked out, ours probably would be too. "Let me try Trina."

Switching gears, I did just that. This time it didn't go straight to voicemail, but there still wasn't an actual answer.

"They're probably out beating Matt and Gray's asses in a snowball fight or something and left their phones in the house. We should be there in like ten minutes. I'm sure everything is fine."

"Yeah, you're probably right."

I may have joked about ditching the trip and barricading ourselves at the lodge last night—and okay, this morning too—

but the truth was the closer we got to the cabin, the more excited I became about seeing my girls.

The last few weeks had been so busy we'd barely seen each other for real. Kamille essentially dedicated all her time to her students once they got back from their Thanksgiving break, which was hectic since they'd had a ton of curriculum to get through before winter break hit on top of having to prep for their Winter pageant, which ended up being cute as fuck.

And then there was Trina, who'd been ducking my calls for weeks. The excuse was she'd been working on some extra important women's fragrance ad project, but even at her busiest, we were usually able to make time to video chat on *Survivor* Wednesdays. Not lately, though. And okay, yeah, I had my own shit going on at the firm now that I was finished with my sabbatical and taking on a full caseload, but damn, couldn't a girl get a little love from her friends?

"Shit, there it is." Izaiah's words pulled me from my thoughts just in time to see the gorgeous cabin coming up on the horizon.

With the fresh layer of snow covering not only the grounds around the property but the trees that framed it as well, the place looked like a bona fide winter wonderland. The effect was even more amazing up close, but one thing was missing.

My lips formed a pout as Izaiah pulled in next to Grayson's truck. "Where's that snowball fight you promised me?"

"Chill with your spoiled ass," he chuckled. He gestured toward footprints off in the distance that looked like they went around to the back of the house. "My guess is they're taking a break to avoid freezing their asses off."

Not a bad idea. Now that he'd shut off the truck, it felt as though the heat had been drained almost immediately. Yeah, let me get my ass in this house and quickly.

I waited patiently as Izaiah climbed out and made his way over to the passenger side door. There was no point in me arguing that I could open my own shit and save him the trouble this one time. Anytime I even looked like I was about to open a door on my own, the man acted like he was about ready to pop me. I'd learned my lesson and I wasn't about to complain.

He placed a quick kiss on my nose after helping me find my footing on the ground and then grabbed the bags out of the back seat while I hefted my backpack purse onto my shoulder.

Entering the code into the front door was simple enough, the warmth of the house pulling me as soon as we stepped inside. As I took in the entryway, it almost had me wanting to redo all of the decorations I had at home. Almost, but not quite.

Izaiah let loose a whistle behind me. "Damn, this shit is nice." Nice was an understatement. I turned to see his face twisted in confusion. "It's quiet as hell, though, for it to be four people in here somewhere."

His words made me pause. He was right. Kamille alone was loud enough for five people and Grayson could never stay quiet even as a kid. Where was everyone?

Almost as if the universe heard me, a noise came from deep inside the house. "Well, someone's here."

I started in the direction the sound had come from only for it to be followed up with another one, louder than the first. This time I could make out voices. Trina and Matt's, if I wasn't mistaken.

"Surprise, bit—*ahhhhh!*"

My feet wouldn't move. They wouldn't move and apparently I couldn't close my eyes either, though it probably wouldn't have helped in the first place since I suspected the image in front of me would be burned into my brain for the rest of my life.

Okay, maybe not that long, but at least for the next few months.

Trina was sitting right in front of me, ass planted firmly on the counter with her legs spread as Matt stood between them, back to me and fingers planted firmly somewhere the laws of the universe said they should not be.

"What the fuck?!" My voice was unrecognizable as I hollered from the entrance of the kitchen. With its open concept and my vantage point, I could see everything. There was nowhere for them to hide.

"I know," I started, voice shaking with disbelief. "I just know that's not Matthew Bellamy Powell standing in the middle of this goddamn kitchen with his fingers buried knuckle-deep in my best friend's coochie. Ain't no way that's what I'm seeing right now."

The realization must have hit him that he'd been frozen in place, Trina's hands on his shoulders almost as if she'd been holding him there, because as soon as the words left my lips they were scrambling apart. As fast as they tried to move, it wasn't nearly fast enough for me, especially once he paused to help her straighten out her clothes, shielding her from view to give her a bit of privacy from me and Izaiah, whose presence I could feel beside me.

"Shit."

Was that all the nigga had to say? With what was unfolding in front of us, you'd think he'd be a little more articulate.

"Is this why no one is answering their phone around this bitch?" I asked. I could feel the hostility radiating off of me as guilty looks settled over their faces.

"Dezireé, we thought…I thought… Didn't you say you wouldn't be here for another couple hours?"

My gaze zeroed in on Trina. "Oh, is that what's happening here? When Dezi's away, the niggas and hoes will play?"

"Dezi…" Matt started, but I held up my hand as a new presence came running into the room.

"Tini, are you o— Dezi!"

Kamille was wearing an oversized shirt, curls spilling out of a messy bun looking like she'd just rolled out of bed. Or just been rolling around in it.

"And you!"

Her eyes widened in shock as she pointed to herself. "Me?"

"Yes, you! What the hell were you doing while these two were in here defiling the fucking countertop?"

"Defiling the…"

Her words trailed off while her brain tried to catch up with my question. I turned back to Trina and Matt, still not believing my eyes. It took about thirty seconds for the scene in front of her to register.

"Tini, you didn't," Kamille groaned.

"Oh, apparently she did." I turned to look at her. "Want to tell me why you seem more surprised by my being here than the fuckshit these two have got going on?"

Somebody had some fucking explaining to do.

izaiah

"AYE YO, what's with all the noise?"

While Zee was busy trying to figure out what the fuck her group of friends had going on, my best friend was walking into the kitchen, completely oblivious.

"Don't start," Kamille said, scrambling to grab both Dezireé and Trina by the hand and leading them out the room.

"When did y'all get here?" Grayson continued, ignoring her. Nah, that wasn't quite right. Did it qualify as ignoring someone if your eyes were glued to their ass as they walked away?

Fuuuuck. Suddenly the reason behind Kamille's current outfit of choice made a whole lot of sense when I combined it with the fact that Gray looked way too goddamn pleased with himself.

"You two really know how to fuck up a trip, you know that?" And here I was thinking that the weather on the way up was going to be what threw this whole shit off. Fooled the hell out of me.

I shook my head at the thought as I stripped off my coat and tossed it onto a chair. "We should've just kept our ass at the lodge like Zee said." Shit was looking real hectic around here and it was going to take a miracle for it not to fuck up my girl's mood. No matter what she'd said last night, walking in on your best friend and your ex was the type of thing no one wanted to see.

Not only had Zee been right about the vibes she'd been picking up from Matt and Trina, but apparently all that bickering her brother was doing with her other best friend was the result of some serious sexual tension. The kind I was ninety percent sure they'd spent the morning, afternoon, and maybe even half of yesterday working out.

Though baby girl was probably too focused on the former at the moment to do the math on that last part. It was only a matter of time before she did, though, and once that happened, shit might really hit the fan.

"What are you talking about?" Grayson asked. "What did I do?"

I know this nigga wasn't actually both offended and confused. Ain't this a bitch?

"You gonna stand there and act like you ain't fuck Kamille?" No point in beating around the bush.

I ignored Matt choking on the water he'd just taken out of the fridge. He'd clearly missed that memo, which shouldn't have been a shock since he'd been up to his own shit for the last twenty-four hours.

"I'm not standing here acting like anything. I just walked in the goddamn room and you starting shit with me. Damn, a nigga can't get a 'hey'? A 'how you doing'? Just diving straight into my business."

"I see you ain't denying it, though." For someone who was quick to tell people what he was and wasn't about to do or hadn't done, he seemed to be focusing on the wrong shit. That told me every-thing I needed to know. Instead of saying anything, he just sucked his teeth and shook his head. I waited, not feeling the need to say another word because I didn't need to. The nigga always told on himself in the end.

Not even a full two minutes later, he was proving my point. "Okay, fine. Maybe I got some cutty last night." He paused. "And this morning. And possibly twenty minutes ago."

Matt and I looked at each other, neither of us knowing whether to laugh or groan at his words. "Bruh, you watch entirely too many movies. Why would you say it like that?" Matt asked, settling on a happy medium between the two as he shook his head.

"I like to keep the people entertained. I'm just trying to figure out why Zay thinks he knows my life or some shit."

"Because the word 'subtle' is nowhere in your vocabulary, nigga. Shit, with the way you were watching Kamille when they left the room, I thought you were about to hump her fucking leg and beg her not to go."

Gray snickered as he waved me off. "Stop being so dramatic. It's like talking to Dezi. If it was so obvious, why the hell you call me out on it but Matt didn't? Shit, I'd be willing to bet he wouldn't have even suspected shit if you hadn't opened your big ass mouth." He crossed his arms, leaning against the island counter.

Matt started to answer, but I cut him off before he had the chance. "That's only because he was too busy trying to get swallowed up in the floor after getting caught in his own mess." Despite—or maybe because of the situation—a laugh found its way up from my chest. "And while we're on the subject, make sure you start by wiping down that counter you had shorty spread out on. I swear neither one of y'all niggas has a lick of home training."

Says the nigga who fucked his woman for the first time on top of her best friend's washing machine. And literally just fucked her in the car yesterday.

That was neither here nor there. My choices weren't the ones up for judgment.

"Daaamn, nigga. When I told you to figure your shit out, I didn't mean do it out in the open where my sister would see!"

"Man, fuck you, Gray. We didn't get caught on purpose. The shit just sort of happened. How were we supposed to know they'd walk in at that exact moment?" Matt rubbed the back of his neck, looking sheepish.

"Carried away when you should've been carrying your ass upstairs to a room." There was no heat to his words, and it was clear he wasn't surprised to hear what we'd walked in on. What had these niggas been doing up here while we were stuck on the road? Conspiring on how to get some pussy in the most unconventional way possible?

Again, pot meet kettle.

"Don't tell me you knew about this shit. And you couldn't give me a heads-up?"

"If you don't calm your ass down. Damn." Grayson did a quick check around the corner. When he was satisfied with what he saw—or I guess didn't see—he gestured for us to follow him to the enclosed porch around back.

The ladies had clearly moved their discussion to another part of the house as well—a bedroom if I had to guess, which was even better. They had some shit they needed to handle and having us within earshot would've just complicated things.

Once we settled in, I looked around in appreciation. "Damn, it's nice out here."

"And heated too," Gray boasted. "Which we found out yesterday while Trina and Kami were making snow angels."

"You're telling me because…" I swear his ass loved to drag out a fucking story.

"Impatient as fuck. Another quality you and my sister share. Damn, y'all really might be made for each other after all."

Jackass.

"Anyway, we were out here enjoying the warmth and the view when I noticed that Matt here was feeling Trina a little more than just as a friend. You think my ass is obvious? This nigga got me beat. Practically drooling."

"Once again, Grayson, fuck ya."

This time, both Gray and I snickered.

"Okay, so what's up? Y'all got up here in this cozy ass weather and just decided this was the perfect time to try some shit out?"

"Not exactly."

I waited for Matt to elaborate, which he looked like he didn't really want to do. At first I thought it was because he figured we would start clowning the fuck out of him. Once he started talking, it was obvious that wasn't the case.

I wasn't expecting him to admit to sleeping with her just a couple months ago. That being the last time they'd really interacted up until now made for an awkward ass car ride and trip, I was sure. It made me wonder why Trina even agreed to come in the first place if she was so hell bent on avoiding him. It wasn't hard to piece together why he'd come, though.

It was the only surefire way to get her attention. And the look that came over his face whenever he said her name during the story told me he craved her attention just as much as I craved Zee's.

"Okay, so this nigga's in love and just isn't ready to admit it," I started, causing Matt's eyes to buck out of his head. "What's your excuse?"

Grayson just shrugged, a smile forming on his lips. "Nobody fucks you as good as a woman who claims to hate your guts."

deziree

MY MIND WAS REELING as Kamille dragged us out of the kitchen and down a hallway into a bedroom I assumed she'd claimed for herself.

"Why is it so fucking cold in here?" Trina muttered, rubbing her hands together.

"Oh my bad, I ummm..." Kamille scurried over to close the window. "I had to handle some business in the bathroom and I figured that would air it out in here quicker."

Okay, eww. TMI.

Not wanting to dwell on that little piece of information for too long, I stood there, gaze shifting between the two women. "Somebody better start explaining some shit real fucking quick before I lose it."

"Oh, was all that hollering you were doing in the kitchen supposed to be the calm version of you?"

Any other time Kamille's little remarks would be cute, but not today.

Instead of acknowledging her, I focused my energy on Trina. "You know, walking in on my ex playing with my bestie's coochie wasn't exactly what I had in mind when I planned this trip. Or when I sent off my Christmas list to Santa." Santa's elves needed to go back to the drawing board. I shook my head as I started pacing. "I mean, sure, I figured something was going on between y'all, but not…that!"

"What do you mean yo—"

"Oh, come on, like your ass has ever been able to keep a secret from me. You've been as cagey as hell the last couple of months. Silly me, I thought it was because your crush on Matthew was back after spending all that time with him recently. It's why I was pressing y'all out to come on this trip in the first place. My Christmas gift to y'all. A little flirting on a picture-perfect vacation, but I guess that was pointless since y'all have been fucking around behind my back this whole time anyway."

"We haven't, though!"

I tooted my lips up in pure disbelief. "You sure? 'Cause that little performance had the two of you looking real comfortable with each other."

"That was…" Trina paused as she tried to pull her words together. "Not a mistake necessarily, even though we could've found a better place to do it. And okay, it wasn't the first time either, but I swear this hasn't been going on consistently. Matty and I only slept together one other time besides this weekend."

"Oh, so you've been bumping uglies with my ex while I was stranded and left for dead on the other side of the mountain, but just one little time before that. Cool. Glad we could clear that up." I had no clue what to do with the energy I was feeling. Part of me wanted to smack her while the other half was telling me to smack myself.

See what happens when you don't mind your fucking business?
asked a voice that sounded suspiciously like Izaiah's.

"Girl, if you don't sit your ass down and shut up!" Kamille
snapped, apparently fed up with my attitude. What the fuck was
her problem? I had a right to be upset that my friends had been
fucking lying to me and I told her as much.

"I'm not saying your anger isn't valid. Nobody likes being lied
to, babe, so I get that. But if you don't close your mouth and stop
with the dramatics, you're never going to hear the full story. And
left for dead where? You were literally cuddled up nice and cozy
with your nigga for the night, probably getting your back blown
out."

Okay, and…

What was her point?

"Also, the high and mighty act about whatever they were doing
in the kitchen is real cute coming from the bitch who laid it low
and spread it wide on top of my washing machine."

I kissed my teeth. "Now why you bringing up old shit?"

"'Cause it ain't that old, boo." Kamille snickered before rolling
her eyes. "And stop pointing out the fact that you and Matty used
to date. That's not breaking news to anybody in this room, so we
don't need the reminder. In fact, weren't you the one who, just a
few months ago, was literally begging us to stop mentioning the
shit?" She cleared her throat. "*Y'all, we broke up over a year
ago! Will you stop bringing it up? It's irrelevant now. We were all
friends first, remember?*" Tilting her head to the side, she shot
me a look.

"First of all, I do not sound like that." Though I might have said
something along those lines. And okay, I may have said it more
than once, but that was irrelevant! "And second, I'm just laying

out the facts here!" I sat on the bed, trying my hardest not to pout.

Trina threw her hands up in exasperation. "Okay, fine. You want to deal in facts?" She took the few steps needed to close the distance between us and sat next to me on Kami's bed. "Let's talk facts. Fact one, I've loved you like a sister since the first day we met. I would never set out to hurt you on purpose, you know that. Even if you want to act like you don't right now, we both know it's true. I've been trying to fight these feelings for months just to avoid something like this happening.

"Fact two, the first and only time Matty and I ever had sex was during his birthday weekend."

I gave her a look.

"Other than this weekend," she added quickly. "And even with that, I didn't come up here with the intention of trying to bang his brains out. Hell, I've been avoiding his ass like the plague ever since it happened."

"She did look like she'd rather crawl out the window and ride on top of the hood than sit in the back seat with him on the way up here," Kamille threw in with a small laugh.

"What about Kamille's birthday? Y'all disappeared for a while." And by then, they'd already been spending a lot of time together. Plus the two of them had been acting weird all night.

She shook her head emphatically. "Nothing happened. Someone stepped on my A'Ones, I got pissed and disappeared, he came to check on me."

"Were the feelings already there?"

After a sigh, she gave a slow nod. "They were. At least for me.

But like I said, I had no intentions of actually doing anything about it."

"Well, clearly something happened between then and now to make you stop fighting it because you certainly weren't trying to avoid him out there."

The way Trina started to fidget told me I was right. There was something else she wasn't saying. Something making her even more nervous than the revelation of what was going on between the two of them.

Kamille placed a hand on Trina's shoulder as she looked away. Aww hell. Whatever this other piece was must be pretty goddamn serious if it was taking all this.

"Fact three," Trina started in a voice that was just above a whisper. She took a deep breath and looked back at me, tears forming in her eyes. "I'm...pregnant."

Did she just say...what?! Visions of a pregnant Trina waddling with a wide nose and even wider smile flashed across my mind.

"Dezi. Dezi!"

Kami's voice snapped me out of my daze.

"I'm sorry, you're going to have to repeat that. I started hallucinating there for a second. Did you say I'm going to be a godmother?"

"Girl!" Trina said, laughing even as tears began to stream down her face. "Really?"

I shrugged despite myself. "What? I feel like it's only fair I get first dibs. That's how it works, right? First dibs on the dick, first dibs on the baby."

She shook her head, looking up at Kamille—who was trying to hold back a laugh—and then back to me. "Don't ask me! It's not like I'm an expert at how this type of thing works?"

"Pregnancy or fucking your bestie's boyfriend?"

"Ex-boyfriend! That's a very important distinction. And I thought we weren't going to mention that anymore!"

"Oh, I never said I was included in that. That rule was specifically for y'all. And even if I was, I hereby reserve the right to bring it up as many times as possible." I nudged her with my shoulder. "It's only right since Kamille won't let go of the washing machine thing. Plus, I kind of like seeing you squirm."

Trina groaned, putting her face in her hands. After a minute or two passed, she dropped them, staring at me while biting the inside of her lip. Despite the smiles and giggles of the last few minutes, she was obviously still nervous. Not that I blamed her. Passing a nigga around the friend group, a nigga who wasn't just a one-night stand, was some unconventional shit.

I pulled her in for a hug in an attempt to ease her anxiety, and more than likely a little of mine too. As much as I wanted to hold onto my irritation—which was still valid in my book—hadn't this been my plan the whole time?

I mean, obviously not this *exactly* 'cause ain't no way I thought Little Miss Faithful With Her Birth Control would be someone's mama right now, nor did I think I'd see them in action, but my goal for getting them both here this weekend was so that something magical could happen. And it did. It just so happened the magic took place a little earlier than anticipated.

"So, for the record…you're not mad?"

Unable to help myself—or lie—I pulled away.

"Oh, I'm mad. Pissed, actually." She winced and I could hear Kamille kiss her teeth. "But," I added, "not about you and Matt getting together. I planned on putting my matchmaking skills to use in that department anyway. What's really getting to me, Tini, is the fact you lied to me about it!"

She opened her mouth to respond but I cut her off, already knowing where she was headed. "You may not have flat out told me nothing was going on between you two, but that's only because I didn't directly ask. Keeping this to yourself and avoiding me so you wouldn't slip up and tell me is just as bad."

I'd barely finished before she started nodding her head. "You're right. I know you're right. I should've said something."

"Exactly, put your big girl panties on and tell me you're riding my old dick. It's not that hard."

That earned me a smack on the arm and an eye roll, a sure sign she was getting back to her old self despite the drama. "Now, I'd ask you how was it, but since I've already indulged in that particular delicacy…"

This time she didn't just smack me, she shoved me, almost sending me off the edge of the bed.

"You're sick, you know that?" Trina said, shaking her head, laughing as she did.

"I prefer to say I'm an acquired taste." I covered her hand with mine. "But don't you do no shit like this again, Tini. And I swear if you swing that pussy anywhere near Izaiah, I will fuck you up."

"Damn, it's like that?" she asked, eyebrows sky-high.

"Oh, it's absolutely like that."

After throwing her hands up, she shot me a quick "you got it" and stretched, a weight clearly lifted off her shoulders.

Kami cleared her throat, catching both of our attention.

"Ummm…now that y'all have done the whole kumbaya thing and you seem to be in a better mood, Dezi, would this be a good time to tell you that I may have sorta…kinda…possibly…fucked your brother?"

My eyes nearly bucked out of my head and fell on the damn floor. My friends had truly lost their minds. The low *"biiitch!"* coming from Trina let me know I wasn't the only one shocked.

"I know you fucking lying, bitch." The grimace on her face said she wasn't. "When? How?"

"I don't know, chile. It just happened!"

"How does some shit like that *just happen*? Explain it to me like I'm one of your kindergartners because it doesn't make a lick of sense to me. You literally hate Grayson. What, did you go to beat his ass, slip, and end up bouncing on his dick instead?"

Kami cocked her head to the side, a thoughtful expression on her face. "Actually…that's not too far off from what happened. The second time at least."

"Y'all did it more than once?!"

Trina laughed. "No wonder it sounded like someone was getting their ass beat in there."

As soon as those two very different sentences left our mouths, Trina and I looked at each other and dissolved into a fit of giggles. You truly couldn't make this shit up. I needed to find a camera to follow me and my friends around. We should be getting paid off this type of shit.

izaiah

IN THE FORTY-FIVE minutes since Dezireé had disappeared to have…whatever conversation they were having, I caught Matt and Grayson up on what happened during the last twenty-four hours for us—minus details—and they did the same. Well, not the same since Matt had some explaining to do on how the fuck they'd ended up in the kitchen, while Grayson didn't dive too deep into what happened between him and Kami but gave us enough to know that somehow, *SportsCenter* and no TV in his room had been the catalyst for them getting together. Oh, and he was hoping for a repeat performance tonight. I wasn't too sure about what Kamille would have to say about that but decided to mind my business.

Once it was all said and done, I figured there was no point in wasting time or being any more uncomfortable than I had to be, so after grabbing our bags from where we'd dropped them in the foyer, I took them up to our room to get settled.

I'd just started drifting off to sleep when I felt arms wrap around me, hands under the front of my shirt and a warm body pressed against my back.

"No sirens. Hands don't feel sticky with blood. It's been too quiet to miss any slamming doors. Either things went well or you went into stealth mode, handled business, and you're just now coming in after burying the body."

It was hard to tell if she thought anything I'd said was funny since instead of her usual laugh, she pinched the shit out of my side.

"Smart ass."

"Aye, don't come in here showing out, woman." I shifted, flipping over so we were facing each other and pulling her in until her head was laying on my chest. "There's an empty room available right down the hall. Act up and it'll have your name written all over it."

"Yeah, right," she said with a snort. Why did she never take my threats seriously?

Maybe because she knows your ass ain't doing a damn thing to her unless it involves stretching her legs back toward the headboard.

Sounded about right.

"Ummm, no, it has Grayson's name all over it."

"I wouldn't be so sure about that."

"Oh, I would," she said confidently as she tucked herself into me even more. "Kamille might've let his ass in her door last night, but I'd be willing to bet money she'll lock him out tonight just to keep him on his toes."

The fact she was referencing their situation at all told me Matt and Trina wasn't the only thing that'd gotten hashed out while they were together.

"So you know about that, huh?"

I could feel the shudder as it wracked her body. "In a lot more detail than I ever cared to hear. There should be some shit that's sacred, you know? Like the lack of knowledge a sister is supposed to have about the pros and cons of her brother's stamina." She groaned. "I don't think I'll ever feel clean again after that conversation. Matter of fact, any bleach around here? Might as well try and use it to clean my mind right on up and get that mental image the fuck up out of there."

Laughing at the seriousness of her tone didn't earn me any brownie points, which was fine. Wasn't like I actually needed them. And she wouldn't admit it, but it broke the tension we needed for me to ask my next question.

"And Trina?"

"Oh, I'm going to need something to get rid of that image too. I'm thinking a few shots of whiskey with an apple cider chaser should do the trick."

This woman.

"You know what I mean, Zee."

"Yeah, I know, I know. Dang, can't a girl have a little maturity with a side of deflection these days? Is that a crime?"

I chuckled, kissing the top of her forehead. "Baby girl, be for real."

"I am being for real, though!"

Even her whining was cute. I really was head over heels for this woman. It was blowing my mind. Grabbing one of her thighs, I lifted it, slinging it across my waist to get her as close as possible. One hand settled on her ass, cupping my favorite cheek—the right one because it had just a little more bounce—while I used the other to caress the entirety of the thigh currently resting on me.

Instead of saying another word, I just let the silence fall over us. It didn't take long for her breaths to fall into the same rhythm as mine, her fingers slowly tracing circles over the fabric of my shirt over my chest like she needed to be touching me in the same way that I needed to touch her.

"I had no idea what to do. What the hell was I supposed to say when we walked into the kitchen and saw them like that?" Dezireé started when she finally began to talk again. And damn if I knew the answer to her question. It was quite possible that if I walked in on one of the niggas from the firehouse all over her the way Matt was up on Trina, a nigga would be facing twenty-five to life on the charge I'd catch over that body.

"I'll take your silence as an 'I don't know,' which is perfect 'cause I didn't know either. I just reacted."

A reaction was one word for it. Honestly, I was surprised she didn't try and take somebody's head off.

"If nothing else, at least you know you were right about the tension between the two of them."

"Being right and acknowledging the tension sounds good in theory, but it's a fucking bitch to deal with when the pussy popping is happening right in front of your eyes."

Touché.

"But..." There had to be one. Wasn't there always? And it wasn't just the one I couldn't stop using my hand to squeeze because the softness was doing something to me.

"But," she said, picking up where I left off. "They both deserve to be happy and everyone around here is grown. If you can't be happy for your two best friends when they find each other, then who can you be happy for? I wanted them to find the type of love I have and it turns out they didn't need my help to do it. I made it clear I won't be tolerating any more of that lying ass behavior, though. That'll get both they asses fucked up on sight."

My body froze as I took in her words. The way she'd so casually slipped the word 'love' into that monologue without a second thought set off flips in my stomach. It was the same reaction any time she said it, but this time, in the aftermath of everything she'd discovered today, hearing her use it in that way—as something for other people to aspire to and want in their lives—that shit did something different to me.

"You love me, lil' baby?"

"Ewww, why would you call me that?"

I chuckled, bringing a finger up to tilt her head so she was looking up at me. "You love me, baby girl?"

"Much better," she said, a smile spreading across her lips. The same smile that made my heart skip a beat at least once a day. "And you know I do. You're mine and I'm yours. What? Did you need me to remind you?"

"Need you to? Nah. But does it get even better hearing it every time you say it? Hell yeah."

The kiss I set on her lips was met with a smile. I loved this woman, and if it was up to me, I'd spend every day reminding her for as long as humanly possible. But first...

"You know what I think?"

"What?" Her tone told me that like I'd been when she first walked in, Deziree was well on her way to drifting off to sleep.

"I think you deserve a treat that shows you just how proud of you I am."

That perked her up quick as hell. "Oh, really? And that treat would be…"

"Mmmm, I could show you better than I could tell you."

trina + matthew
epilogue 1

| SUNDAY |

"ABSOLUTELY NOT," Kamille said, smoke practically pouring from her ears as she gave Grayson yet another death glare. "You've literally just been spinning in a circle for the last three minutes. How the fuck was I supposed to get *Ice Princess* from that?"

Gray shrugged, plopping himself down on the couch and reaching for her, only for Kami to swing on him, popping his hand like he was one of her students. Instead of looking offended, he just smiled. "Wasn't she an ice skater or some shit? That didn't look like ice skating to you?"

We all looked at him like he'd just told us the sky was green. "Bruh, you can't be serious," Izaiah said, which sparked a fit of laughter from everyone except Kamille. I honestly couldn't tell if he was just pretending to be horrible at Winter Movie Charades to annoy Kami or if he was really that bad.

"We're switching partners. Now!" she demanded.

"Nah, no takebacks. Sorry, beautiful." This time when he reached for her, she didn't resist, just pouted as she leaned against him.

This thing between them was weird as hell. I didn't know if I'd ever really understand it, but then again, I guess I didn't need to. Not when my situation was what it was.

"That was the last round anyway, Kami." I held up the whiteboard with the totals and cleared my throat. "And unfortunately for you, y'all are in last place with a total of four points." Kamille rolled her eyes as Grayson pumped his fists like they'd won some sort of victory.

"Have fun cleaning the kitchen." He was going to be hearing about that for a while, especially since it'd been his idea for the losing team to handle cleanup.

"And in second place, we have the good, but not good enough combo of Dezi and Zay with a total of ten points." I giggled as they stood and took their bows.

"Which means," Matthew said, taking the board out of my hands and pulling me onto his lap. "Your winners and first ever champions of Winter Movie Charades are me and the most talented charades partner to ever live with twelve points."

Heat crept into my cheeks as I wrapped my arms around his neck, the smile on my face so wide my face was beginning to hurt.

"Booooooo!" came a chorus of voices behind me as Matt gripped my chin, tilting it down to place a kiss on my lips.

"Uh-uh, keep all that gross shit to yourself," groaned Dezi. "With y'all cheating asses."

The kiss ended way too soon for my liking, but I turned anyway, knowing there were plenty more where those came from.

"And how did we cheat?"

"Clear conflict of interest! You're the one keeping score," Kamille said with narrowed eyes, the pout still firmly planted on her face.

"Not for ourselves," I laughed. "So if you want to blame anyone, go right ahead and blame Izaiah."

"Man, his ass is biased." Grayson managed to pull himself away from the distraction he'd found in Kamille's neck as he stood and grabbed a cookie off the table.

"How you figure?" Izaiah looked genuinely confused.

"Of course you're gonna help that nigga Matt win the game! Anything to make sure the nigga who *used* to date your girl keeps his attention on his new woman and off Dezi." He took a bite out of the gingerbread man. "Matter of fact, sis, you gotta get your lick back. You just gonna let him hand the game to your man-stealing bestie like that?"

I don't think I've ever seen Kamille or Dezi move as fast as they did to smack him. It happened at lightning speed while Zay just chose to flip him off, sending a quick *fuck you* his way.

"What, too soon?" he snickered.

"Nigga, get in there and wash them goddamn dishes. How about you worry about that?" Dezireé gave him another shove as she kissed her teeth. "I'm finna start putting *only child* back on my Christmas list, I swear."

He grumbled something about niggas not being able to take a joke as he headed into the kitchen, Kamille fussing at his ass the entire way. I swear that man said whatever came to mind without a second thought.

"Let me apologize for my messy ass brother." Dezi shook her

head as she stood and yawned. "I'm pretty sure my parents found him somewhere and there's no real blood relation."

I laughed because it wasn't the first time I'd heard her spout that theory. "Girl, Grayson has literally been the same nigga since we were kids. Ain't nobody paying his ass any attention."

I stood as well as she pulled me into a hug. "And besides, it's going to take a while for this not to be completely awkward, right?"

"If you say so."

Dezi swore up and down that seeing me and Matty together didn't bother her once the initial shock wore off. I wasn't so sure since, good relationship or not, only a day had passed since she'd walked in on us in the kitchen. Was that something you could let go of so quickly?

"I do say so, just like I'm going to say ignore Gray's ass. If you're happy, I'm happy." There was no irritation in her voice or skepticism in her eyes. Only a smile right before she peppered kisses all over my face.

"Okay, girl, okay!" I squealed. "Save some of that for your man."

"Mmmm, you're right." She turned, and even though I could only see her profile, I saw the wink she gave Izaiah clear as day before she took off toward the stairs.

He chuckled, shaking his head before dapping up Matthew, who I hadn't even realized was standing beside me, before going after her.

"Does this mean we should wait awhile before we head up? Give them a head start?" I laughed.

"Works for me." His hand wrapped around mine. "Come on, I want to show you something."

As he started to lead me toward the back door, I paused. "Uh-uh, Matty. It's cold as hell out there and I don't have any clothes on." My fuzzy pajama pants were warm, but they weren't that damn warm.

"Chill, mama. We're going to the back porch, that's all."

I pursed my lips, skeptical that he was saying anything so he could get me out back and toss me into the snow, but I went along with him anyway because how could I resist that dimpled smile? He could get anything he wanted out of me with that in his back pocket.

True to his word, we settled out on the enclosed porch with me sitting on his lap as we faced the backyard. Thanks to the heater, the slight chill in the air didn't bother me too much. It seemed to lessen even more once Matty wrapped me in his arms, his body heat an extra layer of protection.

"Now what am I supposed to be looking at that can't wait until morning?"

He pointed straight ahead, the floodlight from the house illuminating the backyard. I didn't understand at first, just saw the ruined snow angels Kamille and I had made two days ago with the new ones we'd made with Dezi earlier that day not too far off to the right.

"What are yo—"

I'd almost missed it. The extra snowman standing next to the two we'd already made. There was no question about who made it, considering the top half of it was lopsided and the head was way too big for the body.

"You know what, I think he's even cuter than the one you made yesterday."

He chuckled. "Oh, yeah? And what do you think about his question?"

Question? What question? Standing, I walked to the edge of the room, finally noticing the sign that was hanging around the new addition's neck.

Trina, will you be mine?

I whipped around in both shock and confusion. "When did you have time to make that? How?" Where had I been that I hadn't noticed this before or caught him doing it?

"Pretty sure you're not supposed to answer a question with a question, mama," Matty said as he stood, meeting me where I was, one hand gripping the back of my neck as he pressed our foreheads together.

"Says who?" I whispered, eyes closed as I reveled in the moment, taking in his scent.

This wasn't how I'd pictured this weekend going, not by a long shot, but now that it was almost over, it was hard to imagine it any other way. I was happy. A lot happier than I'd been just a week ago, and I'd finally decided to stop pushing away this brilliant, gorgeous, sweet man. Why not take one last leap?

"I think we can work something out." I found myself smirking as I tilted my head up for a kiss. "As long as you promise to work on your snowman-building skills."

My giggle was cut off by the soft kiss he pressed to my lips.

"Damn, I can't get an A for effort?"

"Depends on how good your powers of persuasion are."

"Hmmm…" Matty said, a heated look in his eyes. "For my girl-friend? I think I can make it happen."

desireé + izaiah
epilogue 2

| STILL SUNDAY |

I JUST KNOW *they're freezing their asses off.*

That was my first thought as I gazed out the window, watching as Trina and Matty chased each other in the snow, running around the snowman I'd caught him building while she'd been taking a nap. Well, Trina and Kamille. We'd all gathered in Grayson's room—the one he hadn't been using since he'd been staying with Kamille—and watched our favorite Christmas specials on the laptop while we snacked on kettle corn and hot chocolate until the two of them passed out. I wasn't too far behind, falling asleep just a few minutes after Trina, only to be woken up forty minutes later by the laughter outside.

The laughter had come from Grayson, who'd been getting a kick out of watching Matty struggle to get the snow family together.

My second thought was about how fucking adorable the two of them were.

Trina shrieked with laughter while a smile seemed permanently etched onto Matty's face. Neither one of them were dressed warm enough to be outside, but I don't think they cared. Not even when Matt tackled her to the ground, trapping her between himself and the cold snow.

"You trying to head out there too?" Izaiah asked as he came up behind me to take in the view. "Can't say my snowman-making skills are any better than Matt's, but I make a mean ass snowball."

"Yeah, I know! I've got a bruise on my ass from this afternoon to prove it."

His laugh earned him a light push because I was so serious. Here I thought I was the one who took snowball fights too seriously, but this nigga declared all-out war before the game had even really started.

"Awww, I'm sorry, baby. Want me to kiss and it and make it better?" He sealed his offer with a kiss on my temple.

"Yes," I said, a fake pout forming on my face. "But first…"

My body didn't want me to pull away from Izaiah, but if I was going to give him his early Christmas gift, then stepping away— even if it was for just a moment—was a necessary evil.

It took a bit of digging since the envelope had gotten shuffled around since yesterday, but I managed to find it before making my way back over to Zay.

"I thought we were exchanging gifts on Christmas, love." He gave me a confused look. "I'm staying in Oakwood this year, remember?" Instead of heading to Philly to see his mom and grandparents, they were coming down to see him.

"Oh, I remember, but this is sort of a 'must use now' gift."

It was clear he was still confused, but instead of asking any more questions, Izaiah simply opened the envelope carefully, pulling out the three printed and folded sheets of paper I'd slipped inside.

"The AU Lodge?"

"Reservations for the AU Lodge," I clarified with a smile. "This vacation may be over for everyone else as of tomorrow, but we're going back to where this weekend all started. For one more night at least." Making the reservations had been easy when I went to check us out at the front desk before leaving. Not immediately telling him and keeping it to myself for another day? That was the hard part.

"You trying to say you want to spend some extra time with me, love?" His words were teasing as he pulled me in, hands immediately finding my booty as he placed one soft kiss on my lips and then another.

"I have to make sure I get you all to myself whenever I can. This place is amazing and I love it here."

"But…"

God, this man knew me so well. Maybe a little too well some days.

"But the peace and quiet we had while we were at the lodge? I want more of it. With you, of course."

"Naturally because I'm that nigga, right?" And while I would've been annoyed with anyone else for saying some shit like that, my man deserved to talk his shit every once in a while.

Everything always felt so right when I was with Izaiah. Like nothing could touch me and nothing could go wrong. Maybe that was why I'd taken the news of Trina and Matthew so well once I'd calmed down. Kamille was the retired crashout of the group —something Grayson would probably need to remember if he was going to survive—but I'd been known to blow up now and then too.

I'd said I missed the peace of the lodge, and I did, but Izaiah brought me a different sort of peace. The kind that settled over my spirit and created a warm glow inside me. One I just knew everyone could see, and even if they couldn't, I knew it was there.

"Baby girl, you could convince me to fly to the moon with you and I'd do it, no hesitation. An extra day or two of vacation? That's light work."

His kiss left me breathless and wanting more. I backed away, grabbing the front of his t-shirt so we stepped together as I moved us toward the bed. "Well, in that case, why don't you tell me exactly what you think I have planned for us for our third leg of the trip?"

The bed was soft, but not as soft as the way he caressed my face, holding my cheek in the palm of his hand as if I was the most precious thing in the world to him. "Why would I tell you, love? We could have so much more fun if I took the time to show you."

kamille + grayson
epilogue 3

| ONE LAST SUNDAY |

"LOOKS like we've got the downstairs all to ourselves."

It was hard not to roll my eyes at Grayson's suggestive tone. "I don't know if you need your eyes checked, but I can clearly see Matt and Trina outside." How they were out there right now when I was sure it was freezing, I'd never know, but it wasn't my business. Besides, my girl looked happy. I loved that for her.

"Okay, and they're obviously preoccupied. My boy Matty is taking care of business." He leaned against the sink, a smirk on his face as I rinsed the dish in my hand. "So I'm thinking now's the perfect time for us to get a little preoccupied ourselves."

Shooting him the stalest look I could muster, I held out the plate. "Make yourself useful and help me load the damn dishwasher."

His eyes held mine for a beat, then two, before he shook his head and took the plate out of my hand. "I see we're back to this shit."

I balled my face up in confusion. "Back to what, exactly?"

"Back to you playing up this routine like you really can't stand my ass."

"I can't." It was that simple.

"Oh, is that why you just spent the better part of twenty-four hours doing splits on my dick? Could've fooled me."

Okay, so maybe it wasn't simple.

"That was…not me. That was vacation Kamille. Better yet, it was up in the mountains, stuck in a snowdaze Kamille. Tomorrow's our last day, so she's about to get the fuck real quick and make room for regular ole 'Grayson can choke for all I care' Kamille." I cocked my head to the side as I handed him another dish. "Hope you had fun 'cause you won't be seeing the other version of me again."

He nodded his head but didn't say a word. Weird. Grayson always had something to say, even more so when he knew you wanted him to shut the fuck up. The feeling of disappointment that hit me when I realized he wasn't going to say some smart shit to me in return took me by surprise. I tried my best not to show it.

"What if I want to keep spending time with both Kamilles once this weekend is over?" he finally asked once the last of the pots were loaded.

Again, he took me by surprise. Spending the last ten minutes or so in silence had me thinking that maybe he would just give up like I'd implied. Which was what I wanted…right?

"I don't know what you mean."

A sound that could've doubled for the buzzer on a game show filled the kitchen. "Wrong answer, try again."

I kissed my teeth. "Who are you to determine what the right and wrong answer is when it's coming out of my mouth?" The irritation was settling right back in again. The kind that made me want to strangle him and had me wanting to shut him up with a kiss at the same time.

"The nigga who's being up front in saying I want a chance to rectify the mistake I made before, Kamille. Let me take you out."

"We really don't need to keep rehashing this, Gray, I'm over it. All that dick riding I did this weekend, as you so eloquently pointed out, helped me work out all those nasty feelings of rejection and attraction that have been circling the drain for the past year. It's out of my system now. I'm good."

Ready to put this conversation to bed—and climb into one myself—I turned to leave, only to have his hand reach out and grab my arm to stop me. "Yeah, well, I'm not."

"As if I give a shit about what you want."

"You wanna talk about shit we've already gone over, beautiful, and yet you seem to be forgetting one very important conversation we had this afternoon. The one where I was playing that pussy like a maestro on a piano."

I snatched away. "Please, please, do me a favor and go back to not saying shit 'cause I swear you don't know what to say out your mouth. What the fuck is wrong with you?"

"Right now, the only thing wrong with me is the fact that you don't seem to remember me telling you I wanted you earlier."

"And you had me!"

"Exactly. And clearly I'm a fiend waiting for another hit because I don't just want this shit for a couple days, Kamille. I really am trying to see where this goes with you."

I opened my mouth to speak, but he closed in around me, backing me up until we were in the walk-in pantry.

"I'm not saying we need to be on some forever shit like the rest of the niggas in here. All I'm saying is why mess up a good thing? We clearly enjoy each other, and despite what your mouth is saying, I'd be willing to bet money that you didn't get enough this weekend either."

"I got enough of your annoying ass to last a lifetime."

"Lie again."

He waited, an amused look in his eyes as I stood there, nothing to say at the moment because he was right. Fuck me, why did he have to be right?

I wanted what I'd said to be true. If he were really out of my system, I'd walk away right now and leave him to pick up the pieces of his ego without a concern in the world.

But Snowdazed Kamille clearly had other plans because she was whispering in my ear to hop on that dick a few more times. For the science of it all, of course.

"So what happens when one of us gets sick of the other?"

"Aww, don't tell me you're worried you won't be able to hold my attention, Kami."

"Nigga, you wish! I'm talking about when you inevitably get on my nerves—like right now—and I decide it's time to push your ass off the tallest building in the area. Then what?"

He shrugged, apparently unfazed by my question. "Then I get on my knees and remind you that you love having me around for more reasons than just having someone to argue with."

My eyes rolled of their own accord, but the edges of my lips threatened to turn up in a smile. "Grayson, making me come can't be the answer every time you piss me off."

"Says who? Seems to me my mouth irritates you more than anything."

"Your mouth and that attitude."

He laughed. "Yeah, well, your attitude does something very different to me, but let's focus on one thing at a time."

We stood there for I don't know how long, waiting for the other to break.

"I want to make something clear. I'm not suddenly in love with you. And I really do mean it when I say more than half the time, I actually want to choke your ass out. But the dick..." My eyes zeroed in on the print in his pants before traveling back up to his cocky face. "The dick *is* superb."

"And that pussy is unmatched. So give me another taste and maybe I'll let you get on your tiptoes and ride this top-of-the-line dick again."

I hated him. Hated him, hated him, and hated him so much. I made sure to tell him that. But unfortunately, not enough to say no.

Whatever Grayson saw in my face as I said it must've been confirmation enough for him to slowly drop to his knees, pulling my pants down with him. Lifting my foot, he placed it on his shoulder until he was eye-level with the most intimate part of me. "That's probably true, beautiful, but you sure as hell don't hate my mouth. And right now, I want to use that mouth for good instead of evil. Just like I'll do every time we end up in this situation. Might as well practice now, right?"

My eyes watched him as his tongue snaked out, licking along my slit.

"So, how about it? You good with that?"

Maybe I should've said no. Maybe it would've been easier to tell him to get up and that whatever we'd been doing this weekend was officially over. We'd both gotten a taste and we could leave it right here.

But…where was the fun in doing what you were supposed to do?

I lifted an eyebrow as I reached down, digging my fingers in his locs and guiding his face toward the place he seemed so eager to be.

"Are you gonna talk about it?" I asked. "Or eat this pussy like you promised?"

A FINAL WORD

I've been sitting on these characters for awhile. Their stories have changed shape multiple times, but in the end they did what they wanted and led me in the right direction. I hope you enjoy them and their messy ways as much as I did.

If you're able, please find the time to leave a rating and/or review on your favorite platform (Goodreads, Storygraph, etc.). They're the best way to help readers find new favorites and so important when supporting indie authors.

To keep up-to-date on upcoming Lady Marie projects, be sure to sign up for the Spice In Your Life Newsletter, join me on Patreon (Lady Marie Affair), check out my linktree, and follow me on social media @ladymariewrites.

To order a signed copy of any of my physical projects, merch, or web exclusives, please visit the Lady Marie Shop at lady mariewrites.com

ALSO BY LADY MARIE

SISTERS & SERENDIPITY SERIES

Worth It (A Fake Dating Novel)

Found Forever (An Established Couple, After the HEA Novella)

SUGARED AND SPICED SERIES

Sugar, Sugar (An Age Gap, Sugar Arrangement Novella)

Sweet Heat (A FFM Age Gap, Sugar Arrangement Novella)

Sugar-Coated Kisses (An Age Gap Insta-love Novella)

Sweet Control (An Age Gap, Sugar Arrangement Novella)

SLEIGH THE NIGHT COLLECTION

After Tonight (A Brother's Best Friend Novella, _Sleigh the Night_ Prequel)

Sleigh the Night (A Winter Shorts Collection)

HOLIDAY NOVELLAS AND SHORT STORIES

With Sugar on Top (A Sugared and Spiced NYE Short)

Sinnamon & Golds (A Lick Back Season, Thanksgiving Novella)

Szn's Greetings (A Sinnamon & Golds Christmas Short)

Resolutions (A New Year's Novellette)